THE LIONESS AND THE LILY

The Earl felt Purilla quiver, and he was aware that her heart was beating frantically.

"I . . . called to . . . you and . . . prayed for you to . . . come and . . . rescue me."

"I heard you," he said. "I could feel you beside me, and I knew you were in danger."

Purilla raised her face to look at him in a puzzled manner and he said very softly:

"You spoke to me with love, and I listened with love. That is why I was able to save you."

As he spoke he pulled her nearer still.

"Y . . . you . . . love me?"

He was very gentle and as his lips touched hers he felt they were like the petals of a lily, and just as lovely.

His lips became more possessive, more insistent, and he knew Purilla responded not only with her body, but with her heart and soul.

"I love you!" he said. "And I will love you from now until eternity, and perhaps in a million lives that will come after this one."

Bantam Books by Barbara Cartland
Ask your bookseller for the titles you have missed

98 THE DRUMS OF LOVE
99 ALONE IN PARIS
100 THE PRINCE AND THE
    PEKINGESE
101 THE SERPENT OF SATAN
102 THE TREASURE IS LOVE
103 LIGHT OF THE MOON
104 THE PRISONER OF LOVE
108 LOVE CLIMBS IN
109 A NIGHTINGALE SANG
110 TERROR IN THE SUN
115 WOMEN HAVE HEARTS
117 LOVE IN THE CLOUDS
118 THE POWER AND THE
    PRINCE
120 FREE FROM FEAR
121 LITTLE WHITE DOVES OF
    LOVE
122 THE PERFECTION OF LOVE

123 BRIDE TO THE KING
124 PUNISHED WITH LOVE
125 THE DAWN OF LOVE
126 LUCIFER AND THE ANGEL
127 OLA AND THE SEA WOLF
128 THE PRUDE AND THE
    PRODIGAL
129 LOVE FOR SALE
130 THE GODDESS AND THE
    GAIETY GIRL
131 SIGNPOST TO LOVE
132 LOST LAUGHTER
133 FROM HELL TO HEAVEN
134 PRIDE AND THE POOR
    PRINCESS
135 THE LIONESS AND THE
    LILY
136 THE KISS OF LIFE

Barbara Cartland's Library of Love Series

ONLY A GIRL'S LOVE
THE BRIDGE OF KISSES
SON OF THE TURK

Books of Love and Revelation

THE TREASURE OF HO

Other books by Barbara Cartland

I SEEK THE MIRACULOUS

The Lioness and the Lily

Barbara Cartland

BANTAM BOOKS
TORONTO · NEW YORK · LONDON

THE LIONESS AND THE LILY
A Bantam Book / March 1981

ISBN 0-553-14503-7

Published simultaneously in the United States and Canada

Bantam Books are published by Bantam Books, Inc. Its trade-
mark, consisting of the words "Bantam Books" and the por-
trayal of a bantam, is Registered in U.S. Patent and Trademark
Office and in other countries. Marca Registrada. Bantam
Books, Inc., 666 Fifth Avenue, New York, New York 10103.

Author's Note

The description of the confusion at Windsor Castle and the other Royal Residences is accurate. On his own initiative the Prince Consort set about reforming the Household and the Court. He realised that a vast amount of money was squandered in the Palaces, yet not one was even adequately run.

He found, for instance, that while tens of thousands of people were provided with dinners every year, only a portion were actually entitled to them. Candles were replaced every day in the principal rooms whether or not they had been used, those removed being appropriated by the staff as a traditional perquisite.

At Windsor Castle, in one average quarter, no less than 184 new brushes, brooms, and mops were bought, as well as 24 new pairs of home-made gloves, 24 chamois leathers, and 96 packing-mats. At one time there were 300 to 400 dusters "scattered all over the Castle."

Prince Albert threw all his efficiency and head for management into the struggle, and by 1845 there had been a considerable reform, but there is no doubt that when he died prematurely he was worn out by his unflagging desire to create order out of chaos.

Chapter One

1841

As the Earl of Rockbrook drove down the drive of the enormous Georgian mansion which had been in his family since the days of Charles II, he felt no pride of possession.

In fact he barely saw it, as, deep in his thoughts, he drove his horses between the ancient oak trees to draw up in front of the steps leading to the front door with its high Corinthian pillars.

One look at their new Master's face told the servants wearing the Rockbrook crested buttons that he was in a dark mood.

They were all a little nervous of him, as he was an unknown quantity.

They had naturally anticipated that the late Earl's only son would inherit the title on his death, and they had not expected that to happen for at least another ten or twenty years.

However, an accident had happened when the Earl and his son, the Viscount, were travelling together in one of the "new-fangled" and, in most people's minds, "dangerous" trains. They both had been killed, and the Earldom had passed to a cousin who had had no expectation of ever inheriting it.

At the age of thirty-two, the new Earl, who had lived a hard life as a soldier with slender financial means, was delighted, if somewhat overcome, by the grandeur of his inheritance.

It was not only his vast possessions and the position which he held in the County which required getting used to, but also his position at Court.

He was actually no newcomer to the protocol which had to be followed at Buckingham Palace and Windsor Castle.

He had for the last year been *Aide-de-Camp* to the General commanding his Regiment, who, because he was a particular favourite of Queen Victoria, stayed quite frequently in the Royal Palaces.

The General had always insisted on taking him with him because, as he had said:

"You have been with me long enough to know my ways, Brook, and not to ask me a lot of damned silly questions. So if I go to Windsor you come to the Castle with me!"

The young officer had taken it as a compliment, although he was aware that the other *Aides-de-Camp* were jealous and complained of favouritism. However, the General was adamant and there was nothing they could do about it.

The Earl was thinking now that what had seemed at the time quite an enjoyable interlude in his Army life had proved to be a snare and a delusion.

He walked across the great marble Hall with its statues of Greek gods and goddesses set in alcoves, and into the magnificent Library where he knew his uncle had always sat when he was alone or there were no ladies in the party.

He thought that later, when he began to make changes in what had "always been done," he might choose a smaller, more comfortable, and certainly warmer room in which to relax.

But for the moment he was prepared to let things go on as they always had, until he was ready to assert his authority and alter things round to his own liking.

Now, when he should have been feeling a positive thrill at knowing he was the owner of the paintings he had just passed in the corridor and the books which ranged from the parquet floor to the painted ceiling, he was conscious only of the darkness that covered him like a fog.

Outside, the spring sunshine made the daffodils a glowing carpet of gold and enveloped the shrubs of syringa and lilac with light.

Ever since he had been a child he had stayed frequently with his father and mother at Rock and had thought it the most beautiful place in the world.

In the heat of India he had dreamt of the cool of the lake when he had swum in it and of the shadows under the trees where the spotted deer lay until he approached them.

He remembered games of "hide-and-seek" along the corridors and in the attics that were filled with forgotten relics of the past, and how the old Butler had taken him down into the cellars and he had thought the cold stone floors and the heavy doors with their huge locks made it seem like a tomb.

Then, unexpectedly and completely out of the blue, when he had never anticipated for one moment that such a thing might happen, he had inherited Rock.

When he had first learnt of the deaths of his uncle and his cousin, he had felt as if someone had dealt him a blow on the head.

Only after the Funeral was over, and relatives who had never given him a thought for years and County dignitaries who previously had never accorded him anything but a distant bow fawned on him, did he realise the difference between being just a member of an important family and being the head of it.

That, unfortunately, was not the only difference.

Even now, after lying awake all night thinking about it, he could hardly credit that a pit of destruction had opened at his very feet and he could think of no way that he could prevent himself from falling into it.

Soon after Christmas the General had been invited to stay at Windsor Castle and as usual he had said
to his favourite *Aide-de-Camp:*

"You will come with me!"

Although the Castle was cold in the winter and
the less-distinguished guests were often extremely uncomfortable, Captain Lytton Brook, as he was then,
had accepted this duty with pleasure.

"We will not stay longer than we have to," the
General had growled, "but I will be interested to see
if the German Consort has made any improvements."

"There are plenty to be made, Sir," the Earl had
replied, and the General had acquiesced with another
growl.

Not only were the rooms of the Castle bitterly
cold, but visitors to Windsor and the other Royal
Residences soon became aware of the extremely ineffi-
cient way in which they were run.

Frequently there was no servant to be found to
show them where they were sleeping, and newcomers
often found it almost impossible to find their way to
bed when leaving the Drawing-Room after dinner.

The Earl had learnt that on one occasion the
French Foreign Minister had spent nearly an hour
wandering about the corridors at Windsor, trying
vainly to identify his own bedroom.

Finally, on opening what he hoped to be the right
door, he had found himself looking at the Queen, who
was having her hair brushed by her maid before
going to bed.

Another guest who was a friend of the Earl's had
told him that he had abandoned the search in despair.

"I went to sleep on a sofa in the State-Gallery,"
he said, "and when a housemaid found me in the
morning, she thought I must be drunk and fetched a
Policeman!"

The Earl thought this extremely amusing and
related it to the General, who capped it with a story
about Lord Palmerston, who for obvious reasons was
called "Cupid."

When searching for the room of a very attractive

lady, he had stumbled into one where the occupant, at the sight of him, screamed for protection, expecting him to be a rapist!

The gossip now was that with the help of Baron Stockmar, the Prince Consort had set himself the formidable task of bringing order and decency to the Queen's Household.

But unfortunately, as far as the Earl was concerned, it was too late.

On that last visit he had gone up to bed having enjoyed not only an excellent dinner with surprisingly good wines, but also the dance that had taken place after it, which had been far more amusing than standing about making desultory conversation in one of the State-Rooms.

He had just finished reading one of the newspapers and was about to blow out the candles beside his bed when the door opened and to his astonishment Lady Louise Welwyn appeared.

For a moment in the candlelight, because she was wearing a white negligé, the Earl thought she was a ghost.

Then as she advanced towards the bed with a sensuous smile on her lips and an unmistakable glint in her dark eyes, the Earl knew that everything he had heard about her was true.

He had been told by his brother-officers that she was in the same category as Lady Augusta Somerset, the eldest daughter of the Duke of Beaufort.

She, as her father had been warned, was a "very ill-behaved girl, ready for anything that her caprice or passions excite her to do."

There was a tremendous scandal when it was rumoured that Prince George of Cambridge, a highly flirtatious but rather timid young man, had given her a baby.

This had subsequently proved to be untrue, but while tongues wagged and the Dowagers asserted acidly that there was "no smoke without a fire," Lady Augusta had faded from the picture and Lady Louise had taken her place.

She was extremely pretty and the Earl would

not have been human if he had not accepted this "gift from the gods," or rather what Lady Louise offered him.

What was more, as he thought cynically later, it was a very cold night, his bed was inadequately supplied with blankets, and the proximity of the lovely young woman certainly made it warmer.

Actually he was surprised at the fire Lady Louise engendered both in him and in herself.

He had had many "loves" in his life, none of which was particularly serious and most of which cooled off quickly.

It was not entirely flickleness on his part but rather because his Regimental duties made it very difficult for him to play the lover except occasionally.

He had certainly not come to Windsor with the thought of having a love-affair.

He had danced twice with Lady Louise after dinner, and although he had thought her attractive, he had actually found the conversation of another of the Queen's Ladies-in-Waiting far more amusing.

But obviously her feelings about him were different.

"I wanted to tell you to come to me," she said frankly, "but it was difficult to talk without being overheard, so I had to find my way here."

Remembering all the stories he had been told of other people's experiences, the Earl could only think it extremely adventurous of her to have undertaken such a task, even in search of a partner in passion.

He stayed at Windsor for three nights, on each of which Lady Louise found her way to his bedroom, and if he felt somewhat exhausted the next day he thought it was well worthwhile.

However, on the last night he had said good-bye without any heart-searching.

"Thank you," he had said, "for making this the most delightful visit I have ever had to a Royal Residence."

She did not reply but drew his head down to hers, and her lips, wild and demanding, aroused him once again.

However, when he was back in the Barracks he had thought that one of the reforms the Prince Consort might well make would be to remove young women like Lady Louise and Lady Augusta from being in constant attendance upon the Queen.

The Earl had found the Queen charming and, in his opinion, exactly as a young woman should be.

He liked the way she was obviously head-over-heels in love with her German husband, and he liked too the fact that she was undoubtedly very young, unspoilt, and anxious to be, as she had said when she was told that she was to be Queen, "good."

He could understand that since the Queen's marriage, the atmosphere at Court had become quiet and dignified, with a respect for formality which was, the Earl thought, exactly what a man required in his own home.

London offered, to gentlemen of leisure and to soldiers when they could afford it, diversions to please every type of erotic taste.

But that was a very different thing from letting what every decent man thought of as the "seamier side of life" encroach on his family life.

As it happened, the Earl, if he was honest, had been shocked by Lady Louise's behaviour, not so much because she was promiscuous and offered him a fiery passion, but because it had taken place in what should have been the sanctity of one of the Queen's homes.

Now he told himself that he was entirely right in thinking that women with loose morals should be barred, whatever their breeding, from contact with respectable women.

He and Lady Louise had both been aware when they said good-bye that they were, as the Earl had said to himself, "ships that pass in the night."

She had made no suggestion that they might meet again, and the Earl, who had a great many duties in the near future, had actually not even thought of her.

He vaguely supposed that they might meet at Balls or perhaps at another house-party, but as far as he was concerned the episode was over, although he admitted that she had certainly added to the more ordinary amusements he had expected to find at Windsor Castle.

Then yesterday, out of the blue, he had been struck by a thunder-bolt when he least expected it.

The Earl had received an invitation to dinner at Buckingham Palace, a semi-State affair which was one of the many entertainments arranged to herald the Season of "Drawing-Rooms," State Visits, Balls, and public appearances of the Monarch.

He thought it rather amusing to be asked now as himself—the Earl of Rockbrook—rather than merely as an officer in attendance on his General.

He was acutely conscious of the aristocratic sound of his title when upon his arrival he was announced in stentorian tones by one of the Royal servants.

The Queen greeted him graciously and with the smile she kept especially for handsome men.

On being presented, the Earl went down on one knee and raised his right arm with the back of the hand uppermost.

The Queen laid her hand on his so that he could brush it with his lips.

On rising, the Earl bowed silently to Her Majesty, then to Prince Albert, before he moved away to look for a familiar face.

He thought how colourful the huge Drawing-Room, which had been redecorated by George IV, looked with the ladies glittering with diamonds and the gentlemen either in uniform or in Court dress, with a claret-coloured coat, knee-breeches, white stockings, black buckled shoes, and a sword.

He saw, with a feeling of pleasure, the Prime Minister, Sir Robert Peel, whom he admired and liked.

Sir Robert could be rather stiff on occasion and was certainly different from his charming and handsome predecessor, Lord Melbourne, but the Earl had an interesting political conversation with him which lasted until it was time for dinner.

He thought the food and the service had improved since the Prince Consort had taken it in hand, and, looking at him sitting at the centre of the table, opposite the Queen, he thought that he had got a good start but that there was a great deal more for him to do.

He was aware that while the ordinary people had now accepted His Royal Highness and were enthusiastic whenever he appeared in public, the upper classes remained wary of him, while the whole Royal Family were still openly antagonistic.

"I wonder what makes him so unpopular," the Earl thought to himself.

He thought it strange that Prince Albert's prudence, his cleverness, his enterprise in the hunting-field, and his talents as a musician and singer, besides his accomplishments on the Ball-Room floor, all aroused dislike and jealousy rather than admiration.

The truth was, the Earl knew, that the Prince Consort, however hard he tried to be English, appeared determinedly and often arrogantly German.

He suddenly felt a sympathy and commiseration for him.

He was far from home and everything that had been familiar, and it was not natural for any man to have to play "second fiddle" to a woman even if she was the Queen of England.

"Marriage, any marriage, could be the devil in such circumstances!" the Earl ruminated.

He thought, as he had often done before, that he was glad he was not married and that life as a bachelor had all the compensations that any intelligent man could want.

"Someday I must have a son," he thought, remembering that he was now the head of a family whose continuity must be assured. But that was a long way ahead, and at thirty-two there was certainly no need for there to be any hurry on his part.

When the Queen and the Prince Consort had retired it was time for everyone to say good-night, and, after having a last word with the Prime Minister, the Earl was moving towards the door when the Duchess of Torrington came towards him.

Wearing an outsize tiara in front of the three white feathers on her head, a veritable cascade of pearls over her ample bosom, and with the train of her gown well over the three-and-a-quarter yards which was the recognised minimum length, she was a formidable figure.

"I was just going to write to you, My Lord," she said formally, "but this will save me from having to do so."

The Earl inclined his head, expecting to receive an invitation. As he did so, he remembered that the Duchess was the mother of Lady Louise, and decided that he would refuse.

"May we welcome you as our guest at Torrington Castle on Wednesday of next week?" the Duchess asked.

The Earl opened his lips to say he was afraid he was already engaged, but the Duchess continued:

"I understand from my daughter Louise that you have a special reason for wishing to talk to my husband."

She gave the Earl a toothy smile and went on:

"He will be looking forward to seeing you, and may I say, my dear Lord Rockbrook, that you have made me very, very happy."

She patted the Earl on the arm with her fan, then moved away, leaving him stunned.

For a moment he thought he must be mistaken in what he understood her to mean. Then he knew that there was no mistake and he was in a position from which he could see no possible way of extricating himself.

The Duke of Torrington was of great importance in Court circles, the Duchess was an hereditary Lady-of-the-Bedchamber, and if they had decided—or rather if Louise had decided it for them—that he was to be an acceptable son-in-law, there was nothing he could say or do except to make Louise his wife.

The Earl was aghast at the idea. For one thing, while she might arouse him passionately, he did not particularly like her as a person, and she was in no way the type of wife that he envisaged as eventually sitting at he end of his table and bearing his children.

Thinking it over, he knew exactly what he required of the woman who would bear his name.

Firstly, she would be a beauty and have a presence. She would be tall, dignified, and capable of doing justice to the Rockbrook diamonds.

Secondly, on considering the hypothetical wife to whom he was not yet prepared to give a name, the Earl was certain he would not wish to marry anyone who aroused in him the sort of emotions which he considered rather embarrassing.

He would have to have an affection for his wife—that was obvious. He would treat her with the greatest propriety and do his best to protect her from any worries and domestic problems which might arise.

He supposed he had always felt, ever since he was old enough to think about it, that the women to whom one accorded respect were very different from those with whom one enjoyed one's lighter moments.

In the Countess of Rockbrook he required exemplary behaviour, a lady in the fullest sense of the word, and someone who would be a complement to himself.

He knew that Lady Louise could be none of these things. He was aware that he was by no means the only man who had enjoyed her favours and was quite certain that when they were married she would behave in the same audacious manner as she had at Windsor Castle.

> *"Ready for anything that her caprice or passions excite her to do."*

It had really been said of Lady Augusta, but it was no less true of Lady Louise, and he was absolutely appalled at the thought of marrying a woman for whom, if he was honest, he had less respect than for a prostitute who walked Piccadilly as soon as it was dark.

"What am I to do? In God's name, what am I to do?" he asked himself.

He had left London very early in the morning without coming to any conclusion, thinking that somehow he would feel safer when he was at Rock.

But now it seemed only to accentuate his disgust and fury at having to instal Lady Louise in his ancestral home as his wife.

He threw himself down in a chair in the Library and stared at the colourful leather covers of the books as if they could supply an answer.

The door opened and the Butler came into the room followed by a footman carrying a tray of drinks.

"Luncheon will be ready, M'Lord, in a quarter-of-an-hour, but I thought Your Lordship might care for something to drink."

"I will have a brandy," the Earl said.

He usually would have asked for a glass of sherry or Madeira, but he was feeling so heavy-hearted that he needed something very much stronger, although nothing was strong enough to take away the menace that threatened him.

When he was alone, he told himself he must take some course of action, although he was not certain what it could be.

He could of course refuse to accept the Duchess's invitation and go on refusing to have the expected talk with the Duke until Lady Louise gave up the chase.

Yet he was well aware that she was quite capable of informing her father and mother that he had seduced her when they were at Windsor.

That would start the same type of scandal and quarrel that had taken place between the Duchess of Cambridge and the Duke of Beaufort when it was rumoured that Lady Augusta Somerset was pregnant.

There had been in that case some grounds for the rumour, false though it was, but Prince Albert had firmly believed it to be true.

Both he and the Queen refused to speak to Lady Augusta when she appeared at Court and ordered the Ladies not to do so either.

When finally he was solemnly assured that the

story was unfounded, the Prince had answered that he "supposed therefore they must believe it was so."

This had left the Cambridges "by no means satisfied" and the Beauforts "boiling with resentment and indignation."

The Earl could imagine nothing worse, at the beginning of his new life as head of the Rockbrook family, than to suffer the same type of scandal and gossip about himself and Lady Louise.

Yet the only alternative as far as he could see was to fall into the trap she had set for him and marry her.

What made it even more infuriating was that he knew that if he had not inherited the title, she would never have given him another thought.

The Duke of Torrington would never have accepted a penniless, even if well-connected, young Army officer as a suitor for his daughter, but the Earl of Rockbrook was, to put it vulgarly, a very different "kettle of fish."

The Earl felt he was in the same danger he had once experienced on the Northwest Frontier of India, when he and a small platoon had been surrounded by savage tribesmen and heavily outnumbered.

They had known that all they could do was wait for an inevitable and bloody death.

The Earl and his men had actually been rescued at the very last moment, but now he could see no relieving force, nor any hope of one on the horizon.

"What can I do?"

The words seemed to repeat and re-repeat themselves in his brain like the tick of a clock telling him that time was moving relentlessly towards the moment when he would have to write to the Duchess in reply to her invitation.

Last night he had managed to collect himself enough to say in what sounded a somewhat strangled voice:

"It is extremely kind of Your Grace. May I let you know definitely if I can be available on Wednesday?"

"Of course," the Duchess replied with once again that toothy smile.

"But if you are engaged on Wednesday, then of course we shall welcome you on the first possible day you are free."

The Earl had wanted to say that would never be, but the Duchess added archly:

"I know how anxious you are to be with Louise, as she is with you."

Fortunately she had not waited for his reply but had moved away, and feeling as if his legs could barely carry him, the Earl had walked in the other direction.

Now he left the Dining-Room and, completely oblivious of what he had eaten or drunk, deliberately walked through the long range of Drawing-Rooms on his way back to the Library.

They were all extremely impressive, even though like the rest of the house they were somewhat stiff in their arrangement and a little too Museum-like in their display of the treasures collected by the Brooks over the centuries.

It flashed through the Earl's mind that what was needed was a woman's touch, and then he felt himself shudder.

Because his aunt had been dead for ten years, the house had gradually begun to look very masculine in its formality.

This, he told himself, was what he liked. He did not want a woman at Rock. He did not want a woman chattering to him, demanding his attention, and most of all, God knew, he did not want Louise with him in his bed.

He threw himself down in a chair. Then he decided that he could not stand the misery of sitting there thinking of what was to happen.

He must move, he must take exercise. He must do anything but remember Louise's passionate kisses, the fire she had ignited in him which now in retrospect made him feel only disgust.

He rose to his feet, pulled at the bell, and when a servant answered he said he required a horse.

"I want the most spirited horse in the stables."

"Very good, M'Lord. Will you require a groom to attend Your Lordship?"

"No. I will ride alone."

He went upstairs to change into his riding-clothes, and he knew that Bates, his Army batman for some years, was aware that he was in a black mood and had no wish to add to it.

The Earl did not speak until he had changed. Then he said:

"I do not know how long I shall be out riding, Bates, but if I am late returning I do not want everyone sending out search-parties for me. I am quite capable of looking after myself, as you are well aware."

Bates grinned.

As a well-trained servant he knew better than most people how well the Earl could look after himself and those who had served under him.

"I'll keep 'em from worrying about you, M'Lord," he replied.

But the Earl was already on his way along the corridor that led to the stairs.

When he mounted the stallion that was waiting for him outside the front door, it was with some difficulty since the animal was extremely skittish and bucking provocatively.

The Earl had hoped that being in the open air would clear his head and help him to find a solution to his problem, but for the moment he was concerned only with controlling the stallion and enjoying the age-old tussle between man and beast.

He gave the horse its head after they were clear of the trees in the Park and galloped across country at a speed which made it impossible to think of anything but the demands on his horsemanship.

It was a satisfaction to his body if not to his brain.

Only when finally his horse was prepared to settle down and move at a comfortable pace was the Earl confronted once again with the problem of marriage.

Why, he asked himself, had he ever been stupid enough to be inveigled into making love, if that was the right word for it, to an unmarried girl?

He had in fact had little choice in the matter, yet he supposed he could have sent Louise away unsatisfied, even though he would have felt pompous and a prig if he had done so.

Always in the past his love-affairs had been with sophisticated married women who knew the rules and certainly made no attempt to break them.

That was not to say they would not have been eager to do so had it been possible.

It was inevitable, because he was good-looking and an exciting, ardent lover, that women gave him their hearts, even though he merely desired their bodies.

"I love you, oh, Lytton, I do love you!" women had said again and again in his life.

He had been gratified and grateful. At the same time, he could never remember wanting these relationships to be permanent, nor had he found any difficulty or even regret in having to say good-bye.

"Beware of ambitious mothers with marriageable daughters!"

How often had he been told that? And the girls he had met in India had been, as he well knew, the females to avoid.

It was his father who had made his attitude towards the weaker sex very clear from the moment he left Oxford.

"I'm sending you into the Grenadiers, Lytton," he had said to his son. "It is the family Regiment, and I would be ashamed to see you serving in any other."

"I am very grateful, Sir."

"So you should be!" his father said. "You will find you cannot afford any extravagances, and that means watching out for women who charm the guineas from a young man's pocket."

"I will remember your warning, Sir," Lytton Brook said with a smile.

"You cannot afford to marry, but I will say to you what my father said to me," his father went on: "Love 'em and leave 'em! That is good advice, and far less expensive than a wife!"

The Earl had laughed at the time but he had always remembered his father's advice.

Not that ambitious mothers took much interest in him. They always had a pretty shrewd idea of what a man's income might be, and a penniless Subaltern was not an attractive proposition either for a girl or for her mother.

Now the Earl knew that as the holder of an ancient title and acknowledged to be an extremely wealthy man, he had immediately become the prey of every scheming female who wanted a husband either for herself or for her daughter.

But Lady Louise had passed the winning-post while the rest of the field were still under starter's orders, and he was not even to have a chase for his money.

"She has caught me, hook, line, and sinker," he thought savagely, and once again was aware that there was nothing he could do about it.

Because he felt a surge of fury rush through his veins he brought his whip down on the stallion and felt him start more with indignation than with pain.

Then, as if he thought he would teach his rider a lesson, the horse broke into a headlong gallop and the Earl knew he was going to have difficulty in holding him.

However, there was no point in trying to check the animal, so he settled down to enjoy once again the wild rush through the air.

There were trees ahead and the Earl hoped that the horse would not go so close to the overhanging branches that he might be swept from the saddle.

Then unexpectedly when he was still in full gallop the stallion stumbled and the Earl knew that he had caught his hoof in a rabbit-hole.

There was a frantic moment when he struggled to keep his horse on its feet and himself in the saddle.

Then, almost quicker than thought, he found himself falling, felt the impact as he hit the ground and heard the crack of his collar-bone breaking.

Chapter Two

The Earl felt as if he was moving slowly down a long, dark corridor. Then he heard voices and thought he must be waking from a deep sleep.

"You must rest, Nanny," a voice was saying. "You have been with him all night, and I will take your place while you have a few hours' sleep."

"I don't like leaving you, Miss Purilla, and that's a fact!" a sharper, more mature voice replied.

"I am sure I am quite safe."

"That's as may be, but it's not correct for you to be sitting at a gentleman's bedside, as you well know."

"As he is unconscious and has no idea whether I am a woman or an elephant, I cannot believe that it matters."

"I knows, Miss Purilla, what's right and what's wrong."

"What is right, Nanny, is for you to go and lie down. Otherwise you will collapse, and then what will we do?"

"That's the last thing that will happen."

"Why will you not be sensible, Nanny?"

"I'll do as you say, Miss Purilla, on one condition —that if the gentleman wakes you'll come and fetch me at once."

"I think, like Rip Van Winkle, he will sleep for a hundred years!"

There was a sound suspiciously like a snort, as if Nanny thought Purilla was being frivolous.

Then there was the sound of a door closing, and slowly, conscious of an aching head, the Earl opened his eyes.

As he did so he remembered falling because his horse had caught a hoof in a rabbit-hole.

"I must have had concussion," he thought.

He saw that he was in a room he had never seen before.

His bed had a brass end to it, the ceiling was low, and the sunshine was coming through a diamond-paned window.

There was someone standing at the window looking out, and the sunshine seemed to glint on a golden head and a slim body was silhouetted against the light.

Vaguely the Earl thought this must be Purilla. Then he shut his eyes again and drifted away into a comfortable, dark unconsciousness.

＊　＊　＊

When the Earl woke again, the sunshine had gone and it was dark except for a candle beside his bed.

Then as he stirred, there was a firm hand behind his head and a glass was held to his lips.

He realised that what he was drinking tasted of lemon and, he thought, honey, while a firm and authoritative voice said:

"Now go back to sleep!"

It was a voice similar to one that had ordered him about in his childhood, and he knew this was "Nanny" whom he had heard speaking earlier in the day, or perhaps it was a longer time ago.

Because he was very tired he obeyed what he recognised as a command and slept.

＊　＊　＊

It was morning and now he awoke with a feeling of alertness and with an anxiety to know what was happening.

He remembered being given something to drink the night before, and the conversation he had heard, and going back further still he remembered galloping across the field recklessly because he had been angry and had incited his horse into a headlong gallop.

He had "come a cropper," as his grooms would say, and he had no-one to blame but himself.

Looking round him, he saw that the bedroom he was occupying was empty and he wondered where the devil he was.

Then he looked down and saw, to his consternation, that his arm was in a sling, and he remembered that when he had fallen he had been sure he had broken his collarbone.

He moved tentatively, felt the pain shoot through him, and knew he was right. He *had* broken his collarbone, and it was likely to be extremely painful and uncomfortable for some time.

The door opened and somebody came to his bedside, and he knew without being told that this was Nanny, who had been looking after him and ordering him about just as his own Nanny had done years ago when he was a small boy.

She looked down at him and he saw that she was a grey-haired woman past middle-age. She had a kindly face and, at the same time, an air of authority which every child recognised.

"You are awake, Sir?"

"Yes," the Earl replied. "Tell me where I am."

"Where you've been these last three days, Sir. At the Manor at Little Stanton."

The Earl vaguely remembered that it was a small village about five or six miles from Rock House.

"Have I broken my collarbone?" he asked.

"I'm afraid so, Sir, but it has been well set, and as you are in good health, it shouldn't taken long to mend."

The Earl digested this information. Then he said:

"You say I have been here for three days. I suppose I have had concussion."

"I understand when you fell off your horse you landed on your head."

There was just a touch of rebuke in Nanny's voice, which amused the Earl. Then he asked:

"My horse?"

"Very lame, Sir, but being well looked after in our stables."

"I can see I am incumbent upon somebody's kind hospitality," the Earl said. "May I know whose?"

There was a moment's hesitation before Nanny replied:

"This was Major Cranford's house before he was killed last year in India."

"And now?"

"His widow lives here, but she's away at the moment, Sir."

"I thought when I was semi-conscious," the Earl said, as Nanny said no more, "that I heard you speak to someone by the name of Purilla."

He saw Nanny purse her lips together and remembered how reluctant she had been to allow Purilla to take her place at his bedside.

"Miss Purilla," she said in a somewhat repressive tone, "is Major Cranford's young sister."

"I think she has been helping you to nurse me."

"You were unconscious, Sir, when she did so."

"Nevertheless, I am extremely grateful," the Earl said.

It was quite an effort to say so much, and as he lay back against his pillows, Nanny said:

"I'd like to wash you, Sir, and I daresay you could do with something to eat."

The Earl smiled.

"Now that I think of it, I am quite hungry."

"Then I'll order you some breakfast," Nanny said. "Then I'll come back and make you comfortable."

She left the room and the Earl wondered if there were servants to whom she would give the order for his breakfast or whether she was telling Purilla that he was awake.

He wondered what his young hostess was like and thought that, whatever that might be, Nanny obviously intended to be a very conscientious Chaperone.

It was a considerable effort to be tidied up, washed, shaved, and to have his hair neatly brushed and his pillow-cases changed.

Because making a movement, however slight, was so painful, the Earl did not talk but left himself in Nanny's hands almost as if he were a child back in the Nursery.

In fact, by the time she had finished with him he felt so weak that it was an effort to eat the breakfast when it arrived.

"Now eat all you can," Nanny admonished him "You need your strength after being delirious these past days."

"Delirious?" the Earl asked sharply.

"Yes indeed, Sir. It was to be expected, with concussion."

"Was I talking nonsense?"

"Some of the time."

"What did I say?"

"I didn't listen, Sir, but it sounded once or twice as if you were trying to escape from something or somebody."

It was then that the Earl remembered Louise, and he wished for a moment he could lapse back into unconsciousness and be able to forget her very existence.

But once again she was there, menacing him just as she had when she had goaded him into taking a fall while riding a spirited horse.

"Louise!"

He felt that she was there at the end of his bed, jeering at him and making the excellent eggs and bacon he was eating taste like sawdust.

Even so, after he had eaten several pieces of toast with butter and honey and drunk two large cups of coffee he undoubtedly felt more like himself.

Nanny took the tray away.

"Now, Sir, I'm sure you'd like to have a sleep before the Doctor arrives."

"What I would really like is to meet Miss Cranford," the Earl replied, "and make my apologies for descending on her in such an unconventional manner."

"It would be better for you to sleep, Sir."

As she spoke, the Earl saw that she glanced over her shoulder, and he had the feeling that she suspected Miss Purilla was listening outside the door.

He was right, for a moment later the lilting voice he had heard the first time when he had come out of his unconscious state asked:

"May I come in?"

"It's better for him to be resting before he sees Dr. Jenkins," Nanny said crossly.

"He has been resting for days!" Purilla answered as she came into the room.

The Earl looked at her as she approached the bed and was aware that she was curiously like the picture which had already formed in his mind after hearing her voice.

She was very slender, as he had seen when she was silhouetted against the sunlight. Her hair was fair, the colour of the sun when it first arises over the horizon, and her face tapering down to a small chin was dominated by two very large eyes.

They were blue and he thought he would have been disappointed if they had been any other colour, but they had a distinct brightness which took away the insipidity which he usually associated with blue eyes and fair hair.

In fact, she had a lovely face and at the same time there was an attractive mischievousness about her which made her not merely a pretty girl but a distinctive one.

She looked at the Earl and he said with a smile:

"Now you see that 'Rip Van Winkle' is awake!"

She gave the gurgling little laugh he remembered.

"Did you hear me say that?"

"I heard you say quite a lot of different things, but I was still stunned from my fall."

"But you are feeling better?"

"Much better. Please tell me how I was found."

"I found you. In fact, I saw you fall off when your

horse stumbled. The rabbit-holes are very dangerous in that field. I never ride there."

"I should have been more careful," the Earl said ruefully.

"How could you know about the rabbit-holes if you are a stranger? And your poor horse is still very lame."

"It is my fault."

"Ben says that after a strain like that his leg will be weak, and it will be over a month before you can ride him again. Even then you will have to be very careful with him."

She spoke so anxiously that the Earl said:

"You can trust me not to ride him until he is fit."

"It will be some time before you are able to ride yourself."

Purilla sat down on a chair beside the bed, and the Earl, who had heard Nanny going down the stairs while they were talking, now heard her coming up again.

"I am sorry to be such a nuisance to you," he said, "but I am still waiting to hear why, when you saw me fall, you had me brought here."

"Our house was the nearest," Purilla replied, "and really there is nowhere else in the village where you could have stayed, except at the Vicarage with six very noisy children!"

"I am grateful that you played the 'Good Samaritan' rather than the Vicar!"

"Since my sister-in-law is away, Nanny was really rather shocked at the idea of your staying here. But actually she has enjoyed nursing you."

"Enjoyed?" the Earl questioned.

Purilla's blue eyes twinkled.

"She loves having someone to 'baby' as she calls it. I think it is because anyone who is ill is in her power, and although you may protest, you have to do as she tells you."

The Earl wanted to laugh, but he thought it might hurt him to do so, so he merely smiled.

"My Nanny was just the same," he said. "I tried

fighting against her dictates for years without avail, and when I went to School I found the Masters not nearly as authoritative as she had been."

Purilla gave a spontaneous little laugh that sounded very young and attractive.

"I think Nannies are the same all the world over," she said, "and Nanny is very strict with me, even now that I am grown up."

As if speaking of her conjured her up, Nanny came to the doorway.

"Now, Miss Purilla," she said, "I won't have my patient tired out by your chatter."

"I am not in the least tired," the Earl said quickly, knowing that was not quite true.

"You just shut your eyes, Sir," Nanny said firmly, "and you'll find you are asleep almost before you can say 'Jack Robinson'!"

The Earl opened his lips to say firmly that he had no intention of sleeping.

But almost before he realised what was happening, Purilla had been shooed out of the room, the blinds were half-drawn to keep out the light, and he found himself, somewhat to his annoyance, drifting away into dream-land. ...

* * *

It was late in the afternoon before the Earl saw Purilla again.

The Doctor had called and told him he must rest, and Nanny had brought him up an excellent luncheon and told him the same thing.

It was rather infuriating because, although he had no wish to do so, he found that when he closed his eyes he did go to sleep, and in fact when he awoke later he felt more clear-headed and more alert.

Now, when he knew it must be getting on for tea-time, Purilla came into the room carrying a small vase of white violets which she set down beside the bed.

"I was picking violets the day I saw you galloping across the rabbit-field," she said. "There are only small patches of them under the trees and in the woods, but as the white ones are so much rarer than the other kind, I always feel especially lucky when find them."

"I think it was especially lucky that you saw me fall," the Earl replied, "otherwise I might have lain there for days."

"I expect someone would have found you," she replied. "However, as it was, it only took an hour before I could fetch some of the men from the village and they carried you here on a gate."

"I can see I have been a great deal of trouble," the Earl said.

"Actually it has been very exciting," Purilla contradicted. "Nothing much ever happens in Little Stanton, and it has given Nanny and me something to do and the rest of the village something to talk about."

She paused for a moment before she added:

"As you can imagine, they are all wondering who you are."

The Earl smiled.

He was well aware that from the way Purilla spoke, she was as curious as the rest of the inhabitants of Little Stanton.

He was considering if perhaps it would be a wise thing to remain anonymous or perhaps to give a false name.

Then he told himself that, despite what he had said to his valet about no-one fussing about him, by this time they would certainly be anxious and it was only right to let them know that he was in safe hands.

"I expect," he said, "you have heard of Rock House?"

She looked at him quickly.

"Is that where you come from?"

Then she gave a little cry.

"But of course! How stupid of me! I might have guessed! You must be the new Earl!"

"I thought you might have suspected who I am."

"I had heard that a cousin had inherited after the old Earl and his son were killed in a train accident, but somehow I never expected you to be seen in Little Stanton."

"Well, here I am!"

"They must be very worried about you at Rock House."

Her voice was serious as she went on:

"Nanny did look in the pockets of your coat to see if there was anything to identify you in case you were worse than we thought."

"You mean in case I died," the Earl said, "and you wanted to notify the next-of-kin."

Purilla smiled.

"You seemed so big and strong I could not believe that you were seriously injured."

"I am not!" the Earl said firmly. "And I am rather ashamed of being an invalid, especially in a strange house."

Purilla laughed again.

"If we had to have an unexpected invalid drop in on us, I would naturally want it to be a 'tall, handsome stranger,' just as Nanny sees in the tea-leaves when she reads my fortune."

"Does she do that?" the Earl enquired.

"Only when I insist," Purilla replied. "She is Scottish and fey, but she disapproves of playing about with the 'unknown.' It is only occasionally that I can get her to tell my fortune."

"I do not think that would be very difficult," the Earl said.

"Why do you say that?" Purilla asked curiously.

"Because it is obvious that sooner or later a 'tall, handsome stranger,' as you put it, will come into your life even in Little Stanton."

He spoke teasingly and Purilla said:

"Do you know—that has actually happened."

"To you?" the Earl questioned.

He had a strange feeling of something like disappointment as he asked the question, until Purilla replied:

"Not to me, but to my sister-in-law Elizabeth."

Her reply gave the Earl almost a feeling of relief, which he could not explain.

Then he thought it would be a pity if this pretty child, for she was little more, should be forced to lose her illusions too quickly.

"Elizabeth has been very unhappy since my brother Richard was killed, but a stranger has appeared quite unexpectedly and I think, although she is being rather coy about it, that she is going to marry him."

"Surely that is very satisfactory?" the Earl remarked.

While he was listening he was thinking that when Purilla talked, the words were no more expressive than her eyes, which seemed to mirror everything she was feeling and thinking.

"I ... suppose so," she said just a little wistfully, "and I want her to be happy ... but you see ... it is very worrying for me."

"In what way?" the Earl enquired.

"Because Elizabeth and all the people round here seem to think it would be ... wrong for Nanny and me to stay here alone at the Manor."

"You mean that your sister-in-law would move away?"

"Yes, of course, because the man who wants to marry her has a very nice house on the other side of the County. He said I could go and live with them until I am married ... but I know neither he nor Elizabeth really wants me. They want to be alone."

The Earl thought that Elizabeth would certainly not want another woman living with her when she was first married, and certainly not anyone as pretty as her sister-in-law.

It was almost as if he could read in Purilla's eyes the truth of what she was thinking and could understand the problem from her point of view.

Then, as if she felt she was being selfish in talking about herself, she said:

"Do you like being the Earl of Rockbrook? I have always thought it must be a very grand thing to be."

"It is," the Earl said with a smile.

"It must be ... a little uncomfortable for you," Purilla said, as if she was reasoning it out for herself, "coming into the title because of the deaths of two people to whom you were related."

The Earl thought it was perceptive of her to realise this, and he answered:

"It is in fact a great responsibility. That is why, now that I am conscious, you will understand that I must let them know at Rock that I am here, and as soon as I am well enough I must be taken back to my own house."

"There is no hurry," Purilla said quickly, "and if you were moved now it might be very painful."

"Then I hope I may stay a day or two longer," the Earl said. "But is there anyone who could carry a message?"

"Yes, of course," Purilla answered. "I will go myself."

"I cannot ask you to do that."

"I shall enjoy the ride. Although neither of our horses is nearly as well bred or as impressive as yours, they carry Elizabeth and me wherever we want to go."

"I think it would be better for you to send somebody else," the Earl said firmly.

He was thinking that for Purilla to arrive at Rock and say that he was staying in her house would be to invite a great deal more comment, on top of the talk that would be engendered by his accident.

He was quite certain that the fact that she was extremely pretty would not escape notice, and he thought it would be better if the servants could learn of his whereabouts from somebody who looked very different.

"Ben can go, if you prefer," Purilla was saying.

"I think that would be better," the Earl approved. "Now perhaps you would bring me some writing-paper and a pen, and I will write a letter explaining where I am."

He thought as he spoke that he would write to his Estate Manager, a man called Anstruther, who was more or less in charge of everything until he appointed a new secretary. The old one had retired on his uncle's death.

There had been quite a number of important posts left vacant at Rock when the holders had decided that with a change of Master it was a good moment for going into retirement, and the Earl had meant, as soon as he had the time, to go into the matter with his Manager and see who was qualified for the posts.

Purilla brought him the writing-paper and pen he wanted, and because it was difficult for him to write with his left arm in a sling, she held the paper for him and he managed to write a legible letter with instructions as to what he wished to be done.

Then as he signed his name he thought that the best way he could compensate Purilla for the inconvenience of his visit was to provide her with some luxuries which he was quite certain were unobtainable in Little Stanton even if she could afford them.

Accordingly, he added a postscript to his letter asking for fruit from the green-houses and for provisions which he was sure would easily be available, such as eggs and cream.

He also ordered lamb, chickens, and a ham from the Home Farm, which he remembered provided most of the food required at "the big house."

He sealed the letter and handed it to Purilla. Then he said:

"I think when Nanny was going through my pockets she must have found some money and will know where it is now. Will you give Ben a guinea for carrying this for me to Rock?"

"A guinea?"

Purilla was wide-eyed.

"Do you really mean that?"

"I cannot believe, even though I was riding, that my pockets were completely empty," the Earl answered.

"No, no! But Ben will be astonished!"

"Then let us astonish him!"

Purilla gave her enchanting little laugh.

"I do not believe after all that you are a 'tall, handsome stranger,'" she said, "but a Fairy Godfather! If I bring you a mouse, will you turn it into a horse as fine as yours?"

"Are you suggesting that I should have one of my own horses sent over here for you to ride?" the Earl asked.

Because she imagined he was rebuking her, a faint flush rose in her cheeks and she said quickly:

"No ... of course not! I was only teasing!"

"But it is an idea," the Earl said. "I will talk to my valet about it when he arrives."

"He is coming here?"

"I cannot expect Nanny to go on looking after me, and I would not wish to tire her out."

"She will be jealous if you prefer your valet's nursing to hers."

The Earl laughed.

"It makes me feel very important that I should be fought over like two dogs with a bone."

"I am sure Nanny would win."

"I would certainly not bet against it."

Although he would have gone on talking to Purilla for a long time, Nanny arrived to send her off to bed.

Then, almost before the Earl was aware of what was happening, he had eaten a light supper and had settled down for the night.

"If you require anything in the night, M'Lord," Nanny said, "you have only to ring the bell I have put beside your bed. Do not be afraid to ring it loudly. I am just across the passage and I sleep lightly."

The Earl was sure this was true, as she had been used to hearing the cries of children, but he said:

"I hope you have a good night, Nanny, and I shall not disturb you."

"That's what I should be saying to you, M'Lord."

The Earl noted how quickly Nanny had adjusted herself to his title, although he did not feel that it prevented her from still being very firm with him.

"Good-night, M'Lord," she said from the door, "and try to have a real rest while you can."

The way she spoke made the Earl suspect that she thought he lived a riotous, raffish life, and he thought that was actually not far from the truth.

Then when he was alone, almost as if she came into the room as she had at Windsor Castle, Louise was with him again, and he knew the Duchess would be wondering why he had not replied to her invitation.

He felt with a sense of relief that quite inadvertently his visit would have to be postponed whether she liked it or not.

But he knew that what she intended would not be cancelled or forgotten, and Louise would be waiting for him to speak to the Duke.

Perhaps, because he was injured, she would exaggerate her feelings for him still further and pretend a distress at his plight, which her parents would undoubtedly believe.

Louise seemed to come nearer and nearer to the bed in her nightgown as she had done at Windsor Castle when he had first thought she was a ghost.

He remembered the sensuous smile on her lips and the glint in her eyes, which he thought now was that of a wild animal stalking its prey.

It struck him that that described her exactly.

He remembered once a long time ago when he had been in India with his Regiment how he had gone out hunting wild game with another young officer.

As they had not been able to afford the best hunters, they had got lost and at one moment even separated from each other.

The Earl had found after he had shot a deer and several other small animals that he had run out of bullets for his gun and the Bearer had not brought enough with him.

Angrily he told the man to go back to the camp and get some more, and settled down comfortably with his back against a tree to await his return.

It was then that he had been aware that he was in danger.

It was at first only a sixth sense that made him feel almost as if his hair was rising on his head.

But he could see nothing and there was only the quick, frightened movements of birds and other small animals to make him aware that there was something wrong, although he was not certain what it could be.

Then as he got to his feet he knew that the danger had drawn nearer, and he found himself holding his breath, listening, and at the same time looking sharply about him.

Then he saw a young lioness approaching with a feline grace, and he was well aware that she was extremely ferocious and dangerous.

Standing with his back to the tree, the Earl faced her, and while he held an empty gun in his hand he knew he had not a chance in hell of not being mauled and perhaps killed.

Very slowly and almost silently the lioness drew nearer.

Now he could see the gleam in her eyes, the twitch of her nostrils, and the ripple of muscles under her skin as she braced herself to spring.

There was nothing he could do but face her and pray that by some miracle he could fend her off with his gun.

Then unexpectedly, almost as if the hand of Providence intervened and he was not meant to die, a spear, thrown with the accuracy of long practice, came flying through the air from behind him and struck the lioness on the shoulder.

She gave a snarl of pain, then turned and disappeared into the undergrowth.

For a moment the Earl almost fainted with relief.

Then as his Bearer ran up to him and inserted the bullets in his gun, and as the breath seemed to come back into his body, he knew that he had escaped death by a hair's breadth.

Yet no man, he told himself, could expect a miracle to happen not once but twice in his lifetime, and now Louise was waiting for him, encroaching on him, ready to spring, and this time there was no escape.

Morning broke with Bates and all the provisions the Earl had instructed to be brought to the door.

He learnt of their arrival first from Purilla, who almost burst into his bedroom to say:

"How could you have thought ... how could you

have imagined that we wanted so many delicious things?"

"They have arrived?" the Earl asked.

"There is a brake outside filled with food which is now being unloaded into the kitchen, and Nanny is protesting that it is quite unnecessary, while making sure at the same time that she does not send anything back!"

"I should hope not."

"If you eat all that has arrived," Purilla said, "you will be too fat ever to get out of bed."

"I would not wish to starve myself," the Earl replied, "but I want you to have most of it."

"It is very kind of you."

"It is very kind of you to have me here."

"I expect Nanny will try to pretend that you did not think our food was good enough," Purilla smiled, "but I always think it is extremely foolish of people to pretend to be richer than they are, and we are very . . . poor."

"Why?" the Earl asked bluntly.

"Because Richard left quite a lot of debts outstanding when he was . . . killed, and Elizabeth has no money of her own."

Purilla made a graceful little gesture with her hands.

"That is why it will be so exciting for her to marry the rich Mr. Charlton, who is very much in love with her, and she with him."

"That is certainly satisfactory," the Earl said with just a touch of cynicism in his voice. "I suppose she would not marry him for his money if she did not love him."

"No, of course not!" Purilla said quickly. "How could you think she would do such a thing? Although she was poor with Richard, they were very, very happy."

She spoke so indignantly that the Earl said:

"Forgive me. I had forgotten that this is a fairy-tale place and people in fairy-tales always marry and live happily ever after."

There was a mocking note in his voice and also a

bitterness as he thought that that was something which would never happen to him in the circumstances in which he now found himself.

If he agreed to marry Louise he would certainly be unhappy both before and afterwards, and he thought once again as he had last night that she was as dangerous as the lioness had been.

Then he realised that Purilla was looking at him questioningly.

"Why do you speak like that?" she asked after a moment.

The Earl had no intention of being confidential.

"Perhaps I am jealous of such happiness," he replied lightly.

"By that you mean that you would like to marry and live happily ever after?"

"Of course! Surely that is what everybody, both men and women, desire, even if their dreams do not always come true."

"They must for you," Purilla said, clasping her hands together.

"What do you mean?" he asked.

"I was thinking, when you were unconscious and I was watching over you while Nanny slept, that you were everything a man should be."

The Earl raised his eye-brows but she spoke in a quiet serious little voice and was clearly not meaning to flatter him with compliments.

Instead, he was aware that she was thinking it out for herself.

"It is not only because you are ... strong and good-looking," Purilla said, "but also because, although I did not ... know you, I felt you were brave ... good, and kind."

"How could you be so sure of that?"

"That is what I asked myself," Purilla replied, "but I was sure I was right. At the same time, there was something about you that was wrong."

"Wrong?"

The question was sharp.

"It was when you were delirious and talking to yourself. Most of it was nonsense, but I thought you were . . . hating somebody, or perhaps it was a situation . . . I do not know . . . but what you said . . . even though it was not clear . . . you spoke in a tone which seemed to hold both . . . hatred and a sort of . . . disgust."

The Earl was astonished.

At the same time, he knew that she was right in what she had sensed and heard.

He hated Louise, and the thought of her as his wife disgusted him.

"I am . . . sorry," he heard Purilla say quietly in a rather frightened little voice. "It was . . . impertinent of me to tell you what I thought, and I was . . . encroaching on your privacy. Forgive me."

"There is nothing to forgive," the Earl replied.

The light that appeared in her eyes made her look very lovely.

"You must not . . . hate anyone or be . . . unhappy," she said, "because that would spoil the fairy-tale, and perhaps I can be your Fairy God-mother and magic away from you everything that is . . . evil."

She smiled at him in a child-like manner which made the Earl smile back at her in response.

Then as he did so a sudden thought struck him.

Perhaps Purilla could help him? It was not a case of perhaps—she could!

Chapter Three

The Earl was a very methodical man and when he was planning a campaign it had been almost a joke in the Regiment because he was so punctilious about it.

"Brook never loses sight of his objective," one of his Generals had once said, "and the idea of failure or defeat never enters his mind."

Because it had come to him almost like a voice from Heaven, once the Earl realised that Purilla could save him from Louise, he settled down to plan out every small detail.

What was important was that the Duke and Duchess of Torrington and of course their daugher should have no idea that his reason for entering the Estate of Holy Matrimony was to escape from them.

There had been nothing said, he thought, recalling his conversation with the Duchess, which made it imperative for him to explain to her why he could not come to them for a visit as she had suggested.

Her invitation had an innuendo behind it, but that was in reality only because he had a guilty conscience.

He found himself wondering frantically whether Louise, like Lady Augusta, was suspected of being with child, in which case it might be impossible, even by means of marriage to somebody else, to avoid the inevitable scandal.

Then the Earl told himself that if she was pregnant she would have got in touch with him sooner. He had been right in his first supposition that the whole reason for her sudden interest in him was that he had inherited the Rockbrook title and fortune.

Vaguely at the back of his mind he remembered someone in his Club or at a party saying that Louise was having an affair with a man they both knew.

He could not remember now who it was or exactly what was said, but there was no doubt that the gossip he had heard would have been repeated all over London.

He suspected that because Louise was not yet married at the age of twenty-three or twenty-four, she was, in spite of her beauty, growing desperate for a husband, and who more suitable at the moment than himself?

The despair and positive sense of fear which had enveloped him ever since he had left London, and which had arisen again as soon as he had regained consciousness, was beginning to disperse like a mist over the sea.

Now he could see his future more clearly, and there was not the darkness he had envisaged or the slough of despondency from which he had fancied there was no escape.

He lay for the most part of the night thinking over what he should do and what he should say to Purilla.

It made things very much easier that she had no parents, for any mother would think that at least a three-month engagement was obligatory unless the marriage was to appear precipitative and over-hasty.

The Earl had no wish to wait three months or even three weeks to be rid of Louise, and he thought that with his usual good luck, nothing could be more opportune than that Purilla's sister-in-law was to be married and she herself had nowhere to go.

When he fell asleep from sheer exhaustion there

was a smile on his lips, and he awoke feeling that the
world, even before the sun came out, was golden.

When Purilla came to see him later in the morning after he had been washed and shaved and had
eaten a large breakfast, he looked at her in a different
manner from the way he had before.

He had thought then that she was a very attractive, very pretty young girl who amused him by what
she said, and he liked particularly her complete lack
of self-consciousness.

He thought now that this was due both to her
inexperience of the Social World and to her innocence; both attributes which he required in his wife,
especially the latter.

He was sure, watching her as she came across the
room smiling, that her eyes seemed to reflect the fact
that she had no experience of men and certainly had
never been kissed.

There was in fact no comparison between her
and Louise, and he told himself that he was sure
Purilla would always behave with propriety and he
could treat her with the respect that he had always
intended to give his wife.

'She may be a little nervous at first to find herself
the mistress of such a large house as Rock,' he
thought, 'and having continually to visit Buckingham
Palace and Windsor Castle with me. But I will teach
her what to do and what to say, and if she will obey
me there should be no problems.'

He thought how successful he had been in training raw recruits to become good soldiers.

Because they admired him they were eager to
please him, and he had never had any trouble such as
his brother-officers had of their being insubordinate or
obstructive.

Living quietly as she had in Little Stanton and
seeing few people, Purilla obviously admired him, and
because she was so young he would have little difficulty in making her obey him.

In a way it was annoying that he had to marry so
soon after inheriting the title.

If he had had the choice, he would have liked to have two or three years in which to settle down and acclimatise himself to a very different type of life from what he had lived in the past.

But he supposed there was always a penalty of some sort to be paid, and if marriage with Purilla could save him from marrying Louise, then it was something he welcomed, whether it happened immediately or in five years' time.

She came to his bedside to ask:

"Did you sleep well? Nanny said you had eaten an enormous breakfast and would soon be well enough to leave us."

"Nanny must be wanting to get rid of me," the Earl replied.

"I am afraid that is the truth. She thinks you are a disruptive influence."

"On you?"

"I think so. She says all the luxury foods you are providing us with will make us discontented, and although she does not say so, she suspects that when the tall, dark, handsome stranger arrives, I will compare him with you."

The way she spoke was so ingenuous that the Earl was aware that not for one second was she thinking of him as a prospective suitor or even as the Prince Charming that he was sure inhabited her dreams.

It was almost disconcerting, after so many women had pursued him in every part of the world in which he had served as a soldier, and there had always been plenty of female admirers in London when he had the time to meet them.

"You told me that a handsome stranger appeared for your sister-in-law," he said aloud. "I am surprised Nanny did not drive him away."

"She thought him very suitable," Purilla replied, sitting down on the chair by the bed, "and actually he is just the sort of man Elizabeth ought to marry. He is kind and considerate, and he thinks there is no other woman in the world except her."

"I wonder that you did not try to marry him yourself," the Earl remarked.

Purilla looked at him in surprise. Then she said:

"That would have been a sneaky thing to try to do when Elizabeth is older than I am and so very unhappy and lonely without Richard."

Then, as if she was thinking over what he had said, she added:

"Edward is just right for Elizabeth, but he would not suit me."

"Why not?" the Earl questioned.

Purilla thought for a moment. Then she said:

"I think because he is not very adventurous and is a little staid in his ways, and I can guess before he speaks what he is going to say, and I am sure what his opinions will be before he voices them."

"That is certainly somewhat disconcerting," the Earl agreed. "Yet, most women want safety and security in their lives."

"Is that what you have found?" Purilla asked.

If the Earl was truthful, as far as he was concerned they seemed prepared to take extremely dangerous risks with their reputations.

Often when they loved him they became so reckless that they were in danger of breaking up their marriages and being completely ostracised from Society for the rest of their lives.

He realised that Purilla was waiting for an answer to her question.

"I expect that is what they want," he said.

"I do not think you are telling me the truth," she said perceptively. "I am sure you lead a very adventurous, dashing life, and that is what the women who admire you would want."

"You are flattering me," he answered. "How do you know there are any women who admire me?"

Purilla gave a little laugh.

"Now you are being modest, and even Nanny admits that you are a 'fine figure of a man.' That is why she is determined to send you back home as soon as possible."

"Is Nanny afraid that you might fall in love with me?" the Earl asked.

"Of course she is!" Purilla replied. "I can see her growing more and more anxious every day like a clucking hen with one chick!"

She gave her fascinating, gurgling little laugh before she went on:

"Last night when she was helping me undress she said: 'Now don't you go getting ideas about His Lordship. As soon as he's well he'll be going back to Rock, then on to London to the gaieties he'll find there, and which, from all I hears, are very much to his liking. Then you'll never see him again.'"

Purilla imitated Nanny's voice so well that the Earl could almost hear her saying it.

"What was your reply?"

For a moment Purilla hesitated and he thought she might refuse to answer. Then she said:

"I told Nanny: 'His Lordship may forget us, but we shall never forget him. How could we, when he has given us so many delicious things and looks so magnificent?"

"I am delighted you think me magnificent," the Earl said, "but it must be hard for you to judge when you have only seen me laid out unconscious or in bed wearing your father's night-shirt."

The Earl had a childish idea that he would like her to see him in full regimental dress.

Then he thought this conversation might have been written by a playwright even to the point where he would, as the servants would say, "pop the question."

But he told himself that it was too soon, and he knew, by the way Purilla spoke and the expression in her eyes, that while she liked talking to him and admired him, he actually meant nothing personal to her.

Nor did she think of him in what Nanny would undoubtedly describe as "that way."

"What are you going to do today?" he asked.

"I am going riding," she replied. "And I forgot to

tell you how much better your horse is. Ben walked
him round the yard this morning and although he is
still lame he can move quite easily."

"I am glad about that."

"What is his name?" Purilla asked.

"Rufus," the Earl replied.

Purilla wrinkled her nose.

"I think that is an ugly name. One of our horses is
called Mercury and the other is Pegasus."

"I presume you christened them."

"Of course!" Purilla answered. "The moment · I
saw them I thought they were the most beautiful
horses in the world—until I saw Rufus!"

"That is exactly the sort of comparison of which
Nanny would not approve!" the Earl teased. "Now
you are discontented with Mercury and Pegasus and
whenever you ride them you will be wishing you were
riding Rufus."

"I shall do nothing of the sort!" Purilla replied
indignantly. "I admire Rufus, but I love Mercury and
Pegasus, especially Mercury because he is my own
special horse and no-one could ever take his place."

"I can see you are very loyal," the Earl said, but
he did not make it sound particularly a compliment.

"If loving animals and people makes me appreciate them and not feel envious of something that
belongs to somebody else, then I am loyal."

"Which is of course a very commendable quality.
At the same time, I would like to see you riding a
really outstanding horse."

As he spoke, the Earl thought that if she rode
with the same grace as that with which she moved,
she would certainly look outstanding on any horse in
his stable, and he was sure he would want to hunt
with her in the winter.

He had never thought of it before, but now he
decided that his wife should be a good rider.

He had found in the past how bitterly women
who did not ride resented being left behind when
their husbands went hunting without them.

At the same time, he himself was a hard rider,

and he thought it unlikely that a woman would be able to keep up with him.

At any rate, he thought, there would be plenty of things at Rock to occupy a wife, and although he was prepared to give some of his time to teaching her and being with her, he would still be able to keep a great deal of his independence.

It flashed through his mind how much he would enjoy speaking in the House of Lords, attending the all-male parties to which he would be invited, and the very different way in which he would be treated in his Club from how he had been in the past.

There were so many interests now open to him which he could not have afforded before or had not been distinguished enough to take part in.

Most important of all, he was now the owner of a stable with a number of race-horses that were being trained at Newmarket, and he would therefore automatically be elected to the Jockey Club.

He had known when he first inherited the title that the future looked very fair indeed, and it was only Louise who had thrown a dark shadow across the sunshine.

Now that he could see a way out, he felt an upsurge of gratification and triumph in knowing that he could circumvent her plans and even make her look foolish.

The danger before he met Purilla had been very real and, if he was honest, extremely frightening.

Now that was past, and his plans were falling into place with the precision of well-drilled troops.

When the Doctor came he informed the Earl that he should be able to get up in a few days and sit in a chair in the bedroom.

"A broken collar-bone takes time, My Lord, and it would not be sensible to take chances with it, seeing how much there is for you to do."

"So much to do?" the Earl repeated.

"Yes, indeed . . ." the Doctor began, then stopped and looked a little embarrassed. "It is none of my business, My Lord."

"But it is mine!" the Earl retorted. "I should be very grateful if you would finish what you started to say."

"It is not important," the Doctor said evasively.

"I have a feeling that it is to me," the Earl said, "and I would like to hear what is in your mind."

"Very well, My Lord, and I hope you will not think it impertinent. But it is well known in these parts that farming on the Rock Estate is behind the times and old-fashioned. Therefore, we have all been hoping that as you are a young man with a reputation for getting things done, you will give the whole place a good shake-up."

The Earl was astonished.

He had always thought of the Rock Estate as a model of its kind, but then in the last few years when he had been in India he had known very little about it.

His silence made the Doctor look at him apprehensively.

"Forgive me, My Lord, but you did ask me to speak my mind."

"I am glad you did," the Earl replied. "I shall certainly look into everything as soon as I have time, and I promise you I will want modern methods and modern ideas at Rock, as I have wanted them wherever I have been in the past."

"That is what I thought you would say," the Doctor approved. "You will find that in this part of the world there is every possible resistance to change, and you will have to fight every inch of the way. But I think it is worth it."

"I am sure it is," the Earl agreed.

After the Doctor had gone, Nanny insisted that he should sleep, and he therefore did not see Purilla until he had finished his tea.

She told him that she had been riding, then because of what had happened to him she added that she had been particularly careful of rabbit-holes.

"Because Papa could never afford either new farming methods or the men to work them, there are a lot of hazards in our fields."

"I will be very cautious when I am up," the Earl said.

He saw Purilla smile and he knew what she was thinking.

"You have been listening to Nanny again," he said accusingly.

She laughed.

"At luncheon Nanny said: 'Enjoy it while you can. Next week you'll be back to shepherd's-pie and bread-and-butter pudding!'"

"What did you have?" the Earl enquired.

"Roast lamb from Rock and gooseberry fool with cream."

"I had the same," the Earl said. "I thought them both delicious!"

"So did I," Purilla said. "It must be delightful to be able to eat like that every day and accept it as a matter of course."

The Earl wanted to say that was what would happen to her in the future, but he thought that if he spoke too soon he might frighten her, and he also had no wish to make her self-conscious or shy when she was with him.

He had never before been alone with a woman who had not tried to entice him with every allure in her repertoire.

He knew that by this time anyone but Purilla would have been flattering him and making every excuse to touch his hand as it lay on the linen sheets or even to shake up his pillows so that she could be close to him.

Purilla talked happily in her clear, young, lilting voice, and although he felt sure that there was a look of admiration in her eyes, it was the same look that she might have given a fine horse or a beautiful picture, but nothing more.

The following day she came almost dancing into his bedroom with a letter in her hand.

"Elizabeth is engaged!" she said. "They are to be married in three weeks' time."

"You seemed pleased," the Earl said.

"Elizabeth is very happy. She says Edward Charlton is so kind and has given her a sapphire engagement-ring and a brooch of the same stones to match."

"Are you going to be a bride's-maid?" the Earl enquired.

Purilla's face fell.

"No. It is so disappointing! Elizabeth says they are going to be married very quietly in the Church in Edward's village."

She gave a little sigh before she went on:

"I thought she would be married here, but I suppose, as she has not the same ties in Little Stanton as I have, it is more convenient to be married in Edward's Church."

"Where does her own family come from?" the Earl enquired.

"Richard met Elizabeth in India. Her father is a Judge in Calcutta."

The Earl was thinking that this suited him.

It was quite obvious that there would be no-one to interfere or protest when he told Purilla he intended to marry her and take her back to Rock when he was well enough to leave Little Stanton.

When the Doctor came the following day, he pressed him to know how soon he could get up.

"I expect you are growing bored, My Lord," Dr. Jenkins said. "Well, I do not blame you. I am sure you want to get back to your own house, especially when it is a 'new toy,' so to speak."

He laughed at his own joke and the Earl said:

"How soon may I leave?"

"You could go tomorrow, but you would find it a very uncomfortable journey even in a well-sprung carriage. I should give it another two or three days, and even then you will have to be very careful until your collar-bone has knit. If you jar it, it will delay your getting back on your feet—or rather, back in the saddle."

The Earl knew that Dr. Jenkins was talking sense, and he decided to wait another three days.

If he was to be married as he intended before he
left, he knew he would have to tell Purilla immediately of his intentions.

However, before he did so he sent a note by one
of his own grooms to his Solicitors, asking them to
procure him a Special Licence.

He felt it was important that his marriage should
be kept a complete secret, and, knowing that they
were old-fashioned and reliable, he had no fear that
they would talk.

He then decided to speak to Purilla when she
visited him after tea.

He thought it would be pleasant if Nanny would
allow them to have tea together in his room, but when
he suggested it Nanny said that that offended her
ideas of propriety. She said firmly that he should have
his tea brought up and Miss Purilla would eat downstairs as she always did.

"I like talking when I am eating," the Earl grum-
bled.

"That's as may be, M'Lord," Nanny replied, "but
Miss Purilla has got used to eating alone and it's
something that will occur very frequently now that
Mrs. Cranford is to marry again."

"You sound glad about that, Nanny," the Earl
said. "Does it meet with your approval?"

"I think Mrs. Cranford and Mr. Charlton are well
suited to each other," Nanny said.

"And what do you intend to do about Miss Purilla?" the Earl asked. "She is old enough to be married."

Nanny pursed her lips together for a moment,
then she said sharply:

"Now don't Your Lordship go putting ideas into
Miss Purilla's head. She's happy enough at the moment, although in a way it's an unnatural life for a
young girl."

"Why then do you not do something about it?"
the Earl enquired.

"There's nothing I can do," Nanny retorted,
"what with Master Richard being killed just over a

year ago and there being so few young people in the
neighbourhood."

"There must be plenty of them farther out in the
County," the Earl suggested.

Nanny made a derisive sound and he knew she
meant that because they were poor and of little importance, no-one worried about them, pretty though
Purilla might be.

"Well, now that you have one of your charges off
your hands, you will certainly have to do what you
can about the other one," he said provocatively.

"I've always believed that God will provide in
His own good time," Nanny said complacently, "and I
must ask you, M'Lord, not to go upsetting Miss Purilla. She's got her horse, and until you came along
upsetting things she seemed not to be aware that she
was lonely."

"Is she noticing it now?" the Earl enquired.

"I hopes not, M'Lord—I very much hopes not!"
Nanny said in a low voice.

The Earl watched her go with a smile.

What she had said made him aware that Purilla
was already interested in him, and that would make it
easier for her to accept his proposition when he made
it to her.

The more he had seen of her these last days, the
more he thought that the solution to his problem was
a very easy one.

There was no doubt that Purilla was very lovely,
and when she was dressed in the latest fashions in
silks and satins from the best dressmakers, he was
sure that she would be able to take her place beside
any of the ladies at Buckingham Palace.

It would, of course, be wise not to go there too
soon after their marriage, or to Windsor Castle, where
they might meet Louise.

But eventually he would have to present his wife
to the Queen, and he had the feeling that because
they were very similar in outlook, they would get on
well together.

When Victoria had been proclaimed Queen of

England, the Earl had been touched, as had the whole of England, by her grace, modesty, and propriety.

Indeed, Greville the historian had said to the Earl:

"There never was anything like the first impression she produced or the chorus of praise that was raised about her manner and behaviour."

Since the Earl had known Greville for some years and had never found him anything but disparaging about anyone in Society, he had been surprised at his fulsome praise of the Queen.

As the Earl had been abroad when Victoria came to the throne, Greville had delighted in finding someone to whom he could recount what had happened.

Seeing that the Earl was attentive, he had gone on:

"Her extreme youth and inexperience, and the ignorance of the world concerning her, naturally incited intense curiosity."

The Earl felt now, as his conversation with Greville came back to him, that that was exactly what could be said of Purilla.

She was certainly extremely youthful and inexperienced, and, from the conversations he had with her, he knew that she was completely ignorant of the world.

She too would incite curiosity as his wife, especially in Louise, who was waiting for him like a fat spider waiting to devour the fly who had walked into the web she had spun.

'She will be disappointed!' the Earl thought grimly.

He felt triumphant in thinking how clever he had been to circumvent what he now knew was basically a wicked woman.

It was not an adjective he usually used about women, but when Louise had come to his bedroom at Windsor Castle he had known that she was well-versed in the wiles of Satan. Now she had deliberately planned to trap him into marriage, which was undoubtedly an act of wickedness.

Yet, once he produced Purilla there was nothing Louise or her family could do about it.

The thought of how unpleasant the Duke could make life for him at Court if he suspected he was deliberately abandoning Louise gave the Earl a sense of urgency, and he thought that the sooner he married Purilla the better.

He was thinking about her when she came into his bedroom carrying once again a little flower vase carefully in her hands.

"I have brought you something very special," she said.

"What is it?" the Earl asked.

"The first lilies-of-the-valley. There are only six of them, but they smell delicious. Tomorrow there may be more."

She brought the vase to his bedside and held it towards him so that he could smell the delicate white flowers which she had arranged amongst their dark green leaves.

"Thank you," the Earl said. "I think if I had to choose a flower to represent you, it would be a lily, or perhaps a lily-of-the-valley."

He thought she might blush or look a little shy, but instead she said:

"So you think flowers look like people! I have always thought that. Elizabeth is like the small pink musk-roses. We have a bush of them at the back of the house. Nanny, although she gets angry when I say so, is a snap-dragon, rather austere and frightening until you realise that the bees never leave her alone because she has so much honey."

She laughed as she spoke. Then she sat down on a chair and asked:

"Now, what flower do you think you are?"

"I am not interested in myself," the Earl said. "I want to talk to you, Purilla."

"You sound very serious."

"I am," he replied. "Come here and give me your hand."

Obedient as a child might have been, Purilla

pulled her chair a little nearer to the bed and without any embarrassment held out her hand.

The Earl took it in both of his. Then he said quietly:

"We have not known each other very long, Purilla, but I would be very honoured if you would be my wife, and I will do my best to make you happy."

As he finished the speech, which he had prepared while he was resting after luncheon, he realised that Purilla was staring at him wide-eyed with an expression of sheer astonishment on her face.

After a moment she asked:

"Is this a . . . joke?"

"No, of course not," the Earl said. "I am serious, Purilla. I want you to be my wife."

"Why?"

He had not expected the question and now it was his turn to look surprised.

Then he smiled.

"It would make me very happy," he said, "and I have already promised that I will try to make you happy, as I feel you will be."

"Nanny thought that when you left here we would never see you again."

"I am not particularly concerned with what Nanny thinks or does not think," the Earl replied. "I am asking you to marry me, Purilla, and I am sure you would find it an exciting thing to do."

She did not answer, and he went on:

"Rock is a very beautiful house, full of treasures which I am sure will delight you, and although of course there is room for Mercury and Pegasus in my stables, I think you will enjoy riding my horses, which are all as fine as Rufus."

As he spoke, he felt it was extraordinary that she had not accepted him with alacrity, and now it was almost as if he was having to tempt her with other attractions besides himself.

Always in the past, when he had owned nothing, he had thought that when the time came for him to get married, the woman of his choice would accept him eagerly.

And yet now this child, this inexperienced girl living in a very small house in an obscure, isolated village, was not grasping at him as he had somehow expected she would.

What was more, when he was holding her hand it did not tremble or quiver but lay quietly and confidently in his grasp, though he could see a puzzled look in her eyes.

"What is worrying you?" he asked with a faint smile on his lips that most women found irresistible.

"I am trying to understand why you would want me to be your wife," Purilla said. "I know you are very important and that you are often with the Queen and the Prince Consort. I am sure I should be out-of-place in Buckingham Palace, and then you would be ashamed of me."

"You will of course feel strange at first," the Earl answered, "but I will look after you and tell you what you have to do. I promise you that when you get to know the Queen you will find she is not in the least frightening and is very happy with her husband, the Prince Consort, as we shall be."

As he spoke, he remembered the expression of adoration he had seen in the Queen's eyes when she had looked at Prince Albert and the manner in which when anyone spoke about him she told them gushingly how wonderful he was.

Talking to the Earl, who did not often have intimate conversations with her, the Queen had said:

"His Royal Highness is so wonderful, despite the fact that his position is a very difficult one, that I know everyone will do all they can to make it easier for him."

The Earl had merely murmured: "Of course, Ma'am," but he had thought once again, as he had thought before, that the Prince Consort was in a very invidious position.

A man should be Master in his own Castle, and that was something which His Royal Highness could never be.

He was quite certain that that would not occur where he was concerned.

He looked at Purilla now almost impatiently, thinking that by this time she should have accepted him.

"What we will do," he said as his fingers tightened on hers, "is to get married perhaps the day after tomorrow. Then I can take you and Nanny back with me to Rock, because I am quite certain I cannot look after myself without you."

There was a little pause. Then Purilla said:

"The ... day after ... tomorrow?"

"What is the point of waiting?" the Earl asked. "I do not want to leave you, and, as I have said, I need you to look after me until I am well."

"Could we do that? But of course you will have to be very careful of yourself," Purilla said in a different tone of voice.

"It may be rather disappointing that we cannot go on a proper honeymoon," the Earl said, "but I can show you lots of my possessions. Then, once the Doctor allows it, we can, if you wish, go somewhere abroad or to one of my other houses in England."

To his surprise, Purilla rose to her feet, taking her hand from his.

She walked across the room to stand at the window, looking out through the diamond panes as she had been doing the first time he had seen her as he came round to consciousness.

Now he watched her, puzzled and a little bewildered by her behaviour.

He had been so sure that she was in love with him, as much as anyone of her age was capable of being in love.

Besides having no money and apparently very few relations, what woman would not wish to be the Countess of Rockbrook?

Purilla had her face turned away from him and the sun made a halo of gold round her head.

Because he thought it was up to him to take the initiative, the Earl said:

"Come here, Purilla. I want you!"

"I am ... thinking."

"About me—or yourself?"

"Both."

"Well, let me do the thinking. I want you to be my wife, and I cannot believe that you are going to refuse me."

Slowly Purilla turned round.

She walked back from the window. Then as if unexpectedly her doubts seemed to be swept away, she gave him a smile that illuminated her face as she moved swiftly back towards him.

"I think I would...like to...marry you," she said, "but are you quite certain you...want me?"

"Quite certain," the Earl said firmly. "In fact, Purilla, this is the first time I have ever in my whole life asked anyone to be my wife."

"If you had, I suppose you would have been married and you would not be asking me!" she said with unanswerable logic.

"I *am* asking you, and you have not yet given me a proper answer."

He reached out as he spoke and took her hand once again in his.

"It may seem rather a jump in the dark," he said gently, "but I shall be there to catch you."

Purilla drew in her breath.

She seemed about to say something rather serious. Then there was laughter in her voice as she replied:

"You will have to wait until your collar-bone is mended. At the moment it would be very painful for you to catch even a ball of thistle-down!"

The way she spoke made the Earl laugh.

At the same time, it was not really the way he had expected his proposal of marriage to be accepted.

Chapter Four

Purilla ran down the stairs from the Earl's bed-room and out through the side-door towards the sta-bles.

As she neared the stall there was first of all a whinnying from Mercury, then the sharp barks and whining of a dog, followed by scratching on wood.

She opened the door of the empty stall and a small spaniel rushed out like a thunderbolt to throw himself upon her, yelping with delight at her appear-ance and jumping up and down in an ecstasy of joy.

She bent down to pat him and Ben came behind her to say:

"Ye'd think Jason 'ad never seen ye for a month instead of an hour ago since ye brought 'im back!"

"He hates being shut up in the stables," Purilla replied unnecessarily, "but Nanny would not let him disturb our patient."

She did not wait for old Ben's reply, but walked from the stable, followed by Jason, and out across the paddock towards the wood.

She walked quickly, and only when she was in the shadow of the trees did she go more slowly until she reached a fallen trunk and sat down on it, while Jason sat at her feet expectantly, almost as if he anticipated that she would talk to him.

He was not disappointed!

"What am I to do, Jason?" Purilla asked. "He has asked me to marry him, but I have a strange feeling, which I cannot explain even to myself, that he does not really ... love me."

Because she had been alone so much, Purilla had grown into the habit of talking to Jason as if he were a human being who could understand what she was saying.

As if he did understand, he looked at her knowingly with his bright eyes, wagging his tail as he did so.

"I am sure that what I feel for him is love," Purilla went on, as if she was reasoning it out for herself. "He is so handsome, so magnificent, and so exactly what I have always thought a man should be."

She drew in her breath as she continued:

"I want to talk to him, I want to be with him, and when he smiles at me I feel as if my heart is doing ... funny things in my ... breast."

She paused to say in an intense little voice:

"But I want love, Jason, the love I have always ... dreamt about."

Jason made a strange noise in his throat, as if he was trying to answer her.

Suddenly Purilla knelt down beside him on the dry leaves with the green shoots of spring just beginning to show through them and put her arms round him.

"I am ... frightened, Jason," she said. "Frightened that I shall not make him happy ... but more frightened of ... losing him."

Jason licked her face because it was the only consolation he could give her.

Then as she set him free he scampered away to look for the rabbits which he was certain were hiding from him under every pile of leaves and in every sandy hole beneath the trees.

Purilla sat where he had left her, staring across the wood, not seeing the carpet of bluebells in the distance or the last rays of the setting sun turning the trunks of the trees to rusty gold.

Instead, she saw the Earl's handsome face, and heard the note in his voice when he said:

"I want you to be my wife."

It was something she had never expected him to say, and she thought that the words should have made her feel as if she were riding on a rainbow towards the stars.

But somehow, inexplicably, in a way she could not explain to herself, there was something missing.

'He is much older and so much more experienced than any man I have met before,' she reasoned, 'and very different from Edward Charlton.'

And yet she knew that Edward looked at her sister-in-law Elizabeth with an expression in his eyes that told her without words how much he loved her.

Long before he had said anything to Elizabeth about marriage, Purilla had known perceptively that they were in love with each other but too shy to express it.

She thought that just as Nanny was fey, she had been fey where they were concerned.

She could feel their love beating in the vibrations that emanated from them, hear it in the way they spoke of even the most commonplace things, and see it in their eyes as they looked at each other.

That was love, irrepressible, irrefutable, impossible to hide or ignore.

Purilla knew that while the Earl looked at her in a kindly manner and the feeling of his hand on hers was comforting and secure, there was something else which she knew, if she was honest, was essential to her happiness and to his.

But already she had said that she would marry him because he had told her he wanted her.

"I can look after him ... I can help him," she told herself.

And yet deep down inside her, something was saying that it was not enough and that she wanted more, very much more from the man to whom she gave her heart.

* * *

Nanny changed the Earl's bandages and gave him a clean sling for his injured left arm.

He did not talk while she was doing so, for the simple reason that he was waiting to feel the inevitable pain which came when he moved.

To his surprise, there was not only no pain but very little discomfort, and he knew that the bone, which had not been badly broken but only cracked, was knitting and he would soon be on his feet again.

He was well aware that he was exceptionally strong even among his contemporaries, and because he ate sparingly of the right sort of food and drank comparatively little, it was to be expected that his bones would knit faster and heal quicker than would those of a less athletic man.

Nanny finished her task and collected the used bandages to carry them away from the bed.

As she did so, the Earl looked at her face and thought she looked a little more grim and perhaps more disapproving than usual.

"What is the matter, Nanny?" he asked.

"What have you been saying, M'Lord, to upset Miss Purilla?" she enquired.

"Is she upset?"

"She's gone out on one of her walks," Nanny replied, "as she always does when things aren't right or she's got something to think about. And why should she do that when she's just come back from the wood, I'd like to know?"

The Earl smiled at the aggressive note in Nanny's voice before he replied:

"I think perhaps Miss Purilla has gone to think over the suggestion I have just made to her."

"Suggestion, M'Lord?"

Nanny's tone was sharp.

"I have asked her to marry me," the Earl said quietly, "the day after tomorrow."

For a moment Nanny stared. Then as he saw what he knew was an expression of relief in her eyes, she said:

"You intends Miss Purilla should be your wife, M'Lord?"

"I do indeed, Nanny, and I hope to make her happy."

"It's what I'd wished, M'Lord," Nanny said, "but why must the marriage take place in such an unseemly hurry?"

"I thought you, of all people, would understand that I cannot stay here with Miss Purilla unchaperoned, and as I want her with me at Rock, that again would involve difficulties in finding a Chaperone, unless we were married."

Nanny was silent for a moment, as if she saw the logic of this reasoning. Then she said:

"It'll cause talk, M'Lord."

"On the Estate, perhaps," the Earl replied, "but does that matter?"

Nanny considered this, and as she did not speak he thought she was grappling with a desire to be more conventional and at the same time to feel the gratification of seeing her charge become a Countess.

She capitulated.

"I suppose Your Lordship knows what you're doing," she said, "and if Miss Purilla's happy, that's all that matters."

"That is what I thought," the Earl said quietly.

When Nanny left the room he lay back against his pillows, thinking that everything was going according to plan and Purilla had saved him from the danger that had been just as imminent as the danger that moment in Africa when he had waited for the spring of the lioness.

Even now he knew he would not be entirely safe until the ring was on Purilla's finger and it would be impossible for Louise to have any further hold over him.

"I will give her everything in the world she wants," he told himself.

He planned that tomorrow, when Mr. Anstruther

visited him, he would get him to write to London for
the smartest and most expensive dressmakers in Bond
Street to send down their latest creations and to order
a great many more gowns to consitute her trousseau.

It might be slightly delayed, but she should have
one fit for a Princess, which in its own way would
express his gratitude.

Mr. Anstruther had already written, on the Earl's
instruction, a letter to the Duchess of Torrington
which he had composed with care.

Mr. Anstruther had in fact made several drafts
before it was entirely to the Earl's satisfaction. It had
finally read:

> *Rock House*
>
> *Her Grace the Duchess of Torrington*
>
> *Your Grace,*
> *I am instructed to inform Your Grace that
> it is with deep regret that the Earl of Rock-
> brook cannot accept Your Grace's kind invitation
> to Torrington Castle.*
> *His Lordship has unfortunately been injured
> in a fall while out riding, and while his injuries
> are not of a serious nature, he is for the moment
> in the care of the Doctors, who will not permit
> him to travel.*
> *His Lordship has asked me to convey to
> Your Grace his apologies and regrets for not hav-
> ing answered Your Grace's invitation sooner.*
> *I am,*
> *Your Grace's humble and
> respectful servant,
> J. B. Anstruther*

The Earl felt that all the information the Duchess
might require was in the letter, while it committed
him to no further action.

He therefore dismissed the Torringtons from his
mind and wished he could do the same where Louise
was concerned.

He supposed it was his physical weakness which
made him feel she was still there menacing him, still

trying to force him into a situation from which he shrank with every instinct in his body.

"Once I am married, there is nothing she can do," he assured himself again and again.

He found himself wishing that he was not alone and that Purilla would return from the wood.

However, he had to wait quite a long time before he heard her footsteps coming lightly up the stairs.

Then there was a knock on the door and she came in, just as dusk was falling and the last dying remnants of the sun had sunk over the horizon.

And yet the Earl thought that she seemed to light the room with her fair hair that shone like a torch as she came towards the bed.

He realised that she was not alone, and as she moved towards him a dog followed her.

"Who is this?" the Earl enquired.

"I have come to ask you if he may stay with me," Purilla said. "He hates being shut up in the stables."

"Has he been exiled on my account?"

Purilla nodded.

"I am afraid when he is excited or wants something he will bark, and Nanny said it would disturb you."

"That will not matter now, as I am nearly well again," the Earl replied. "What is his name?"

"Jason."

The Earl raised his eye-brows.

"It does not sound quite so romantic as 'Mercury' or 'Pegasus'."

"But it is!" Purilla contradicted. "I called him Jason because he is always searching."

"Of course—for the Golden Fleece!" the Earl remarked.

"That is right."

She sat down on the chair beside the bed and after a moment she added:

"I feel that in a way it is something we all do."

The Earl was fondling Jason's ears and he looked at her for a long moment before he asked:

"And what are you searching for?"

He had the feeling that she was trying to tell him something, but he was not prepared for the colour that came into her cheeks or the shyness in her eyes as she looked away from him.

It made her appear unexpectedly lovely. Then as if she had no wish to answer his question she jumped up quickly to say:

"It is getting dark. I cannot think why Nanny has not brought you the lamp. I will light the candles, then I will draw your curtains."

"There is no hurry," the Earl said. "I am waiting for you to answer my question."

"I . . . I cannot remember what it . . . was," Purilla replied.

"That is not true. You told me that everybody is searching for something, and I am interested to know what you wish to find."

"I suppose . . . everyone wants . . . happiness," Purilla said in a low voice.

The Earl knew that this was only half the answer and he was sure that the word she was too shy to say was "love."

It struck him for the first time that, while he had told her he wanted her and needed her, he had not actually said that he loved her.

He was aware that it was what every woman would expect to hear from the man who had offered her marriage.

He suddenly had the uncomfortable feeling that if he said to Purilla: "I love you!" she would know with her "sixth sense," or perhaps with an instinct which he was aware she used where people were concerned, that it was not the love she was seeking.

A love, he told himself, which was the idealistic emotion she had heard about in fairy-stories and which had little to do with the ordinary world in which they both lived.

"I will respect and protect her, and she shall have everything she wants in the way of diamonds and jewels, and a social position that is second only to Royalty. What more can she ask?"

The Earl felt as if the question was unnecessary and he knew exactly what Purilla was looking for. He was far too intelligent to pretend ignorance when the truth was only too obvious.

'Love!' he thought cynically.

How many aspects of love there were, ranging from the erotic fantasies catered for in London, to the passion that was nothing more than lust which had brought Louise through the labyrinth of corridors to his bedroom at Windsor Castle!

He knew that that was not the love Purilla was seeking, but he told himself that the idealised love which was part of a fairy-tale existed only in her mind and had no reality in the world today.

'I must try not to disillusion her,' the Earl thought to himself.

He knew that what she was demanding of him was not in his power to give and inevitably sooner or later she would be disappointed.

Because in a strange way the idea upset him, he asked himself almost angrily why he could not have met an ordinary, stupid young country girl.

She would be utterly content if a real live Earl had been sent to her like a gift from Heaven and would ask nothing more than that she should be transported into a social position which was almost too dazzling to contemplate.

He felt that this aspect of their marriage was of little or no consequence to Purilla, but how he knew it he was not certain.

He was aware that she was marrying him only because he attracted her. She was, however, still unawakened to any great depth of feeling, though her instinct told her there was something missing in his offer.

Because he felt that to talk of love in a room that was darkening was dangerous, the Earl said quickly:

"You are right, Purilla. Light the candles. Or better still, ask Bates to bring up the lamp. We should not allow Nanny to keep coming up and down the stairs. It is too much for her."

"If I cannot find Bates I will bring it up myself," Purilla replied.

She walked quickly towards the door, and Jason, who had been standing on his hind legs with his head down on the bed in an ecstasy of delight while the Earl stroked his ears, wrenched himself away almost violently to run after her.

The Earl watched them, then as he heard them both going down the stairs he lay back against his pillows and told himself he was being needlessly apprehensive about Purilla.

She was young, adaptable, and, he was sure, very teachable. He would soon get her used to his ways.

Because she was sensible she would not make unreasonable demands upon him or ask him for something he could not give.

"I suppose by her standards I have never been in love," the Earl ruminated.

He thought it strange that Purilla of all people should make him come to this conclusion.

It was in fact something he had never thought about until now. He had been amused, enamoured, and sometimes a trifle infatuated by women who fell all too easily into his arms the moment he showed the slightest interest in them.

Yet he could never remember feeling heartbroken when one of his liaisons came to an end or his Regimental duties took him elsewhere.

There would be an exchange of letters for a short while, which would grow fewer and fewer and finally would cease.

But always where one woman had left a vacuum in his life there was another one to fill it.

'Once we are married she will settle down at Rock,' the Earl thought, his mind back once again with Purilla, 'and when we have children she will have plenty to occupy her.'

Again he thought it was slightly unfortunate that he was being pressured into marriage so quickly after he had inherited.

Then he remembered that the Doctor had said there was a lot to be done on the Estate, and because she had always lived in the country he was sure that Purilla would find it interesting.

After a little while perhaps he could leave her in charge of certain local responsibilities and occupy himself with more serious matters such as politics.

"She will be all right," he told himself in an over-hearty manner which made him know that he was giving it undue emphasis as if to convince himself.

And yet later, before he went to sleep, he found himself thinking of that elusive, sentimental, romantic emotion described as "love," which meant something different to everyone who searched for it.

* * *

Getting into his frock-coat was not as difficult as the Earl had anticipated.

He still had to wear his arm in a sling but it did not prevent him from looking extremely smart when he was finally dressed for his wedding.

It seemed strange, he thought, that his marriage should take place so quietly and there would be no witnesses except Nanny and Bates.

He know, however, that speed was essential, and because a plan had already formed itself in his mind, he had extracted a promise of secrecy not only from Bates but from the Vicar.

"You can understand," he had said to the latter, "that as Miss Cranford has no relatives, it is quite unnecessary to have a large wedding which, being attended only by my friends and relations, might make her feel embarrassed."

"Of course, of course, I understand that, My Lord," the Vicar agreed.

"What is more," the Earl went on, "I am quite certain that had I contemplated anything but a very quiet ceremony, Dr. Jenkins would have forbidden it to take place for several weeks."

The Vicar nodded understandingly, and the Earl continued:

"That is why, as I have to go to Rock House,

taking with me Miss Cranford and her Nurse, I think it wise that we should be married here in Little Stanton and give our explanations afterwards."

The Vicar had been most accommodating.

"I am sure you are right, My Lord, and I agree with Your Lordship that a large wedding is very exhausting, especially for the bride and bridegroom."

As if he had been following his Master's train of thought, Bates said:

"They'll be surprised to learn you're bringing home a wife, M'Lord, and I expect when Your Lordship's better they'll expect some sort of festivities."

"Do you mean a party with fireworks?" the Earl murmured beneath his breath.

"Exactly, M'Lord!" Baes agreed. "Very disappointed they'd be to miss out on what they looks on as their right, so to speak."

The Earl laughed.

"Then we must contrive that they will not be disappointed, Bates, but for Heaven's sake not until I am well enough to endure the strain of it!"

"I'll see to that, M'Lord," Bates said. "The Doctor's put Your Lordship in my charge, so to speak."

"You had better not let Nanny know that," the Earl said. "I am quite certain he said the same thing to her."

Bates grinned.

"I hopes not, M'Lord. I've a feeling she wants to keep you at her mercy!"

"I can quite believe that," the Earl replied.

He negotiated the stairs slowly and cautiously.

He had moved about the room the day before, but this was different.

Although it was only a short distance to the Church there was a carriage waiting outside, and when he reached the Hall, Bates had ready a bottle of champagne on ice to fortify him for the ceremony ahead.

He was drinking the champagne, thinking as he did so that he needed something to give him strength, when he realised that Purilla was beginning to descend the stairs.

He looked up, and, seeing her for the first time fashionably gowned, he thought how lovely she looked.

Nanny had insisted that she should have a new gown even though there was no time to collect one from London.

She had instead taken one of the Earl's carriages and driven to the nearest town, where she had managed to find what Purilla called a "miracle" wedding dress.

While it would not have "passed muster" in St. George's, Hanover Square, it certainly looked opulent enough for a small grey-stone Church in Little Stanton.

It had a very full skirt, an off-the-shoulder neckline, and puffed sleeves ornamented with lace. It was, the Earl knew, a copy of the gowns the young Queen had made the zenith of fashion.

What made it different was the exquisite Brussels-lace veil, held by a wreath of orange-blossom, which fell to the floor in a small train.

It was Mr. Anstruther, on learning of his impending marriage, who had told the Earl of the veil all the Rockbrook brides had worn at their wedding-ceremonies.

"I expect, My Lord, you will require the Rock veil?" he had said.

"I had not thought of it," the Earl admitted, "but I suppose naturally there must be one."

"Of course, My Lord," Mr. Anstruther replied with just a touch of rebuke in his voice. "It has been worn by all the family brides for the last hundred and fifty years, and the wreath, which I am sure Your Lordship will remember, is of artificial orange-blossom inset with diamonds."

This was something the Earl did not recall, but he did not want to confess his ignorance.

However, when the veil arrived from Rock he knew it would be exactly what Purilla would want and would give her the feeling, which he was sure she desired, of being a fairy-tale bride.

As it happened, the moment Purilla saw what she was to wear, her thoughts were of the Earl.

Because even lying injured in bed he appeared so magnificent, she had been afraid that he would be ashamed of her.

Now with her new gown, which she thought could not have been excelled by anything available in Bond Street, and with the lace veil that might have been made by fairy-fingers, and the glittering wreath, she looked very different.

She stared at her reflection in the mirror and prayed in her heart:

'Let him think I am beautiful...please let him think I am...beautiful.'

She had never seen the ladies of the Social World in which the Earl moved at Buckingham Palace or at Windsor Castle, when he was in London, but she had read descriptions of them and seen sketches of the Queen and her Ladies-in-Waiting in the *Graphic* and the *Illustrated London News*.

She was quite certain that she would look like Cinderella amongst them, especially in the simple gowns that Nanny had made for her from the cheapest materials obtainable simply because it was all they could afford.

Now in a gown which seemed to her to be the epitome of fashion, with a veil that made her look as mysterious as a nymph rising from the mist which lay over the stream in the morning, and the diamonds glittering on her head, she felt that the Earl would be proud of her.

Then as she thought of it she knew that that was not all she wanted him to feel.

She wanted him to love her, she wanted him to look at her with an expression in his eyes which would tell her that he gave her not only a wedding-ring and his name but also his heart.

"I want his love...I want it," she told her reflection, and thought the eyes in the mirror looked back at her pleadingly.

In some ways she felt as if the Earl understood her perhaps better than anybody else did.

There had been a tussle with Nanny because

Purilla had insisted that Jason should come with her to the Church.

"He must stay in the carriage outside," Nanny had said decisively.

"I want him to see me married," Purilla insisted.

"It's not right for dogs to be in Church. He'll cause a commotion, and what'll His Lordship say to that?"

"Bates has said he will hold him, and he likes Bates," Purilla persisted, "and I must have one person there who really belongs to me."

She saw that Nanny was about to argue, and went on quickly:

"I shall try to believe that Mama and Papa are there on my wedding-day, and I must pretend that Richard is giving me away as he would have done if he had lived. But I must have something that belongs to me to actually see me married, and that must be Jason."

"You'll have to ask His Lordship," Nanny said when she had not the heart to go on fighting.

The Earl had agreed without any argument.

"Of course Jason can be there if you want him," he had said, "although I think the Vicar would object to Mercury coming into the Church!"

"I thought ... if you did not mind," Purilla said a little breathlessly, "that Ben could lead him as far as the porch, and he would be the first person I would ... greet when I come out with a ... different name."

The Earl smiled.

"Mercury must definitely wait at the porch," he said, "but I think you should be grateful that I do not wish to have all my horses there as well. It might cause a stampede!"

Purilla laughed. Then she said:

"Although I am sure your horses mean a lot to you, it cannot be the same as what Mercury and Jason mean to me. When Richard was killed, they were the only people I could talk to, and they try to understand what I am saying to them."

"Now you can talk to me," the Earl said firmly.

There was a little silence and he understood that she was waiting for him to finish the thought.

"I will try to understand what you are saying to me," he said, "and it should not be too difficult."

Purilla gave a little sigh.

"I am afraid perhaps you will think that . . . some of the things I say are . . . childish and . . . silly."

"Shall I promise you that is something I will never think?"

She shook her head.

"You may find it is a promise you cannot keep, and that would be a mistake. But I would like to be able to tell you things and not be afraid you would . . . laugh."

"That I can definitely promise I will not do," the Earl said, "and I think, Purilla, that as we have not known each other for very long, it is very important that we should talk frankly and openly without pretence and without being afraid of misunderstandings."

"I would like that," Purilla replied. "At the same time, because you have done so much in your life, I do not wish to bore you with too many questions . . . but there is so much I want to learn."

The Earl smiled.

"There are a lot of things I want to teach you. But first, as you must realise, I must get well."

"Of course," Purilla agreed. "Dr. Jenkins gave both Nanny and me a lecture this morning, saying that you were not to do too much or you might have a relapse."

"That is something I have no intention of having," the Earl said, "and it is common sense not to run before you can walk."

It sounded very reasonable, but when they drove the five miles from the Church to Rock, the Earl was aware as they drew near the great house that he was feeling very tired.

He told himself it was because he was weak, and he knew too that apart from his accident, the anxiety he had felt about Louise and the fact that he had not been able to sleep the night before, for worrying about his wedding, had all taken their toll.

He must have looked pale, because Purilla suddenly asked anxiously:

"Are you all right?"

The Earl found it difficult to answer.

She put her hand in his and said to reassure him:

"The journey will not take long."

His fingers closed over hers and he felt himself clinging to her as if she were a lifeline that he needed at this particular moment.

Then the carriage drew up in front of the steps, the red carpet was down, and the servants in their livery and powdered wigs stood waiting.

With an effort, almost as if he were going into battle, the Earl drew himself up as the carriage door was opened.

Then with Purilla at his side they were walking up the steps and into the Hall, where a long line of servants were waiting for them.

The Earl and Purilla shook hands with everyone present before they moved across the Hall and into the great Salon with its silk brocade walls and painted ceiling.

It was decorated with white flowers and Purilla gave a cry of delight at the beauty of it.

Then she heard the Earl say beside her:

"For God's sake, get me a drink, and make it a brandy!"

She heard the urgency in his voice, and, looking at him, she realised that his face was white and drawn.

She looked round her wildly, but fortunately the Butler who had been just behind them heard what the Earl had said.

"The brandy's here, M'Lord," he said. "Sit down; Your Lordship'll soon be all right."

Because he was too weak to do anything but obey, the Earl sank down in the nearest chair, and although it seemed to him a long time, it was in fact only a few seconds before a glass of brandy was put in his hand and he lifted it to his lips.

He felt the fiery liquid coursing down his throat to disperse the darkness that had swept over him, and for a moment it was almost a joy because he had been afraid of falling down and not being able to move any farther.

He drank a little more, then he saw that Purilla was kneeling beside him, her eyes wide and frightened as she looked up at him.

He told himself that he must reassure her.

Then as he prepared to do so, he realised that not only was she looking at him with anxiety but that her blue eyes held an unmistakable look of love.

Chapter Five

The Earl was sitting in the Orangery with a number of papers in front of him when Purilla joined him.

She hesitated before speaking, and he looked up and realised that she was a little shy because she was wearing one of the new gowns he had ordered for her from London.

It was exceedingly becoming and looked what it was—extremely expensive.

He knew by the expression in her eyes that she wanted his approval, and he said, as was expected of him:

"You look charming! Bates told me that a carriage-load of gowns had arrived this morning, and I hope they please you."

"They are wonderful, more wonderful than anything I have ever had before, but I feel a little strange...."

She paused before she added:

"You do really ... like me in this ... gown?"

"You look very lovely," the Earl said. "Is that what you want me to say?"

He saw by the way her face lit up that she had been anxious in case she did not please him, and he thought how vulnerable she was and how his mar-

74

riage was likely to be much more difficult than he had expected.

For the last two days he had felt too tired and too weak to worry about anything except regaining his strength.

After he had almost collapsed on his arrival at Rock, Bates had sent a groom post-haste for Dr. Jenkins, who had scolded the Earl in more or less the same way Nanny had.

"I warned you, My Lord, against overdoing it too quickly," he said. "Concussion is something we know little about, except that the patient should rest and not do too much. You disobeyed the rules and now you have to pay for it."

"All right, all right!" the Earl said irritably. "You have made your point. I will take things easy, but nothing infuriates me more than to feel as I do now."

"Physical injuries are one thing, mental ones another," Dr. Jenkins said, "and I have the feeling that you have not only to cure your body, My Lord, but also your mind."

The Earl did not acknowledge that he was right, but he knew that for a local Doctor, Dr. Jenkins was in fact usually perceptive.

He had been worried—worried about Louise, worried about his marriage to Purilla, even though it seemed such plain-sailing, and worried too about the future with a young girl who did not now seem to him as simple and amenable as he had expected her to be.

The Earl was not conceited, but he was aware that women found him exceedingly attractive, and he had expected that any woman he married would of course love him and be content with the affection he would give her as a husband.

What he had not anticipated was that Purilla would, although she had not said so, demand not affection but love.

He could see by the expression in her eyes when she knelt at his feet that she had fallen overwhelmingly in love with him and that what she was giving him was not only her heart but her soul.

How he knew this he was not certain, and he told himself he was not an imaginative person. But he was aware that he was now part of Purilla's dreams and that the material advantages in their marriage were of very little importance beside the fact that she loved him as a man.

"Perhaps I am exaggerating what she is feeling," he tried to tell himself when he thought about it at night.

But he knew, with an instinct he had seldom used before where women were concerned, that her love was an idealised emotion for which she sought, as Jason had sought for the Golden Fleece.

For the first time in his life the Earl found himself thinking of a woman's reactions to him rather than of his to her.

Always before when he had desired a woman he had made love to her and knew as he satisfied her passion that little else was of any consequence.

But with Purilla it was different, and he had the uncomfortable feeling that if he attempted to make her his wife without the love she demanded of him she would be both shocked and frightened.

"I am imagining things," he said to himself over and over again.

And yet the idea still persisted, and everything she said and did seemed to strengthen his conviction that what he had to offer would not satisfy her.

Now with her eyes shining she came closer to him to say:

"How can I thank you? How can I begin to tell you what it means to have such beautiful clothes and to feel that after all I am not a . . . beggar-maid in the Palace of Prince . . . Charming."

"Is that how you have been feeling?" he enquired.

"Of course," she answered, "even though I have walked about with my eyes shut."

He looked at her, not understanding, and she explained:

"I thought you would want to show me your

treasures yourself. So I have deliberately not looked at the paintings or anything else and am waiting until you are well enough to tell me about them."

It was the sort of sensitivity he might have expected of Purilla, the Earl thought, but aloud he said:

"But of course I want to be your guide the first time you inspect Rock and see if it is really the Palace of your dreams."

"It is ... I am sure it is!"

Her eyes met his as she spoke, and he knew that what she was really saying was that it was he who made the fairy-story real, and the place in which he lived was unimportant except that it was a background for himself.

"Come and sit down," the Earl said. "I feel I should apologise for being so tiresomely indisposed immediately after our marriage."

"It is understandable," Purilla said, "and Dr. Jenkins has been angry with me for letting you do too much too quickly."

"It was what I wished to do," the Earl said, "and therefore I cannot complain or put the blame on anyone except myself."

"But you must be very careful," she said in an earnest little voice. "Dr. Jenkins told me how dangerous it can be for people who fall on their heads, and even the smallest amount of brain-damage may affect one for years."

"I assure you there is nothing wrong with my brain," the Earl said sharply. "In fact I am busy at the moment making plans to improve the Estate, so perhaps you would like to hear about them."

He told himself that it might be a mistake to dwell too long on the subject of their personal relationship.

He therefore picked up the papers he had been reading when she joined him, and she saw that one of them was an adverisement for a threshing-machine.

"Are you really thinking of buying that?" she asked.

"Do you know what it is?" the Earl enquired.

"Yes, of course I do," she replied. "It is a threshing-machine."

"I believe every up-to-date Estate has one."

"I suppose so, but at the same time you must be very careful how you instal it."

The Earl looked at her in surprise.

"Perhaps you were abroad," she said, "when ten years ago there was so much trouble over the installation of threshing-machines that there was a rebellion amongst the farm-labourers."

"I have heard about it, of course," the Earl replied. "But now the labourers have accepted them."

"There are none in this part of the world," Purilla said, "and therefore they will be very frightened if you introduce one, unless you make it very clear that it will not affect their wages."

The Earl looked at her in astonishment.

"How do you know this?"

"There are farms all round Little Stanton, and wherever I walk I am always welcome."

"It surprises me, Purilla," he said, "that you should be interested in threshing-machines and the labourers' reaction to them."

"But of course I am interested," Purilla replied. "I have been told so often of how the labourers fired the stacks and broke up the machines, and how many of them were transported or ... hanged."

There was a little sob in her voice as she said:

"It was a losing battle, but most employers compensated their workmen for the wages they lost when the threshing was taken away from them, and I think now in many parts of England there is not so much suffering or starvation as there was."

The Earl put down his papers.

"I see, from what you are saying, that I shall have to study the improvements I wish to make from a different point of view. I suppose I was just thinking that machines would be more efficient."

"I am sure they are," Purilla said. "At the same time, the farm-labourers rely on the money they earn during the harvest to keep them through the lean months of the year, and on many farms they are very, very poorly paid."

The Earl looked at her sitting in the chair beside him and thought this was certainly not the sort of conversation he had expected to have with anyone who looked so young and who until now he had suspected had a head filled only with fairy-stories.

He was quick enough to understand exactly what Purilla was saying, and he remembered reading of the labourers' rebellions in Kent and Sussex and the other Southern Counties, and how the Government had sent troops to confront the rioters who were fighting to save themselves and their families from starvation.

He realised that Purilla was looking at him with a pleading expression in her eyes, and after a moment he said:

"I promise you that any machinery I introduce on my Estate will not bring any financial harm to my employees."

She gave a sigh of relief as if it meant a great deal to her. Then she said:

"When you have time, I think you should ... visit some of your ... cottages, especially those on the ... north side."

The Earl knew that these were the nearest to Little Stanton, and, knowing the answer, he asked:

"Why?"

"Because they need a lot of repairs done to them, and also, if there are to be innovations, surely you could spare a little money to improve and modernise the homes of those who work for you?"

The Earl gave a laugh. Then as he saw the question in Purilla's eyes he explained:

"I am laughing because I never expected for one moment that I should find I had married a Reformer!"

As the colour came into Purilla's cheeks she said:

"You told me that we should speak frankly with each other, and I have wanted to tell you this for some time, but I waited until I thought you were well enough."

"I am well enough now," the Earl said firmly, "so

tell me everything you know about my Estate."

Purilla took him at his word and told him of the families she had visited and how some of them were forced to have boys and girls of all ages sleeping in one room, while in others young children had to sleep with their grandparents.

She told him too of cesspools which were broken down, roofs which needed mending, and wells which the Doctor felt were contaminated but nothing was done to cleanse them.

She spoke quickly and a little breathlessly, as if she was afraid the Earl would be bored before she had finished all she had to say.

Only when she paused did he reply:

"I am glad you have told me this, Purilla. At the same time, I am wondering why I have to learn the truth from a stranger rather than from my Estate Manager."

"I do not think it is actually Mr. Anstruther's fault."

"Why should you say that?"

"Because I understand, from all I have heard, that your uncle, the late Earl, was not interested, nor was his son, in the people on the Estate. Actually they did not think of them as individuals but only as a means of providing what they required."

The Earl thought that this was very likely true.

He had known that his uncle spent most of his time in London, performing his duties either in the Royal Household or in the House of Lords.

His cousin, the Viscount, for whom he had never had any great liking, had always been intent on enjoying himself either on a race-course or in the company of lovely women.

It was his love-affairs, and there had been a great number of them, that had prevented him from marrying as he should have done and providing an heir to the title.

It had of course been to the present Earl's advantage, as this neglect of duty had resulted in his inheriting.

But now he saw that the task ahead of him was not to be as easy as he had anticipated.

As if she sensed what he was thinking, Purilla said: "Only you can change everything. Only you can put right what has been wrong for a very long time."

The Earl rose to his feet and walked across the flagged floor of the Orangery to stand at the open door and look out onto the garden.

The sunshine was warm, the air was mellow, and the last few days had brought all the flowers into bloom.

Already there was a profusion of lilac and syringa, daffodils and narcissi, and the trees, covered in pink-and-white blossom, gave the garden a young, fairy-like quality that made him think it was a perfect background for Purilla.

And yet, instead of the beauty which he always associated with Rock and which he had carried with him wherever he went in the world, he thought now it was like a drop-curtain at a Theatre, hiding a lot of ugliness behind it.

For the first time since he had inherited he saw it not as a magnificent, enviable possession, but as an obligation to which he must dedicate himself both mentally and physically to achieve the perfection it deserved.

He felt as he had in the past on being handed a Company of raw recruits and knowing it was entirely up to him to make them into an efficient fighting force which would be worthy of the Regiment to which they belonged.

When this happened he had always looked on it not only as a challenge that was part of his duty but as something which brought out his fighting spirit. And now, unexpectedly, that was what was required of him at Rock.

Purilla had not moved, and although he did not turn round he had the feeling that she was waiting apprehensively to know what his intentions were for the future.

It struck him as strange that this girl should have

showed him where his duty lay, and that although she
was younger than any woman in whom he had ever
shown any interest before, she should have sympathy
for the underdog and not be concerned only with
herself.

He turned round.

"Why does it matter to you if these people are not
as well looked after as they should be?"

Purilla smiled.

"Of course I had no idea that I should ever have
a personal relationship with them, but they are people, just like you and me, and it . . . hurts me that they
should not be happy."

"I can see, Purilla," he said, "that you must help
me to cope with my obligations, and as you know so
much more about the countryside than I do, you must
work with me to change things for the better."

He saw the delight in her face and thought that it
might have been aroused by the gift of a diamond
bracelet rather than a promise of what would undoubtedly be quite hard work.

"What else have you to tell me?" he enquired.

Purilla was about to tell him about some other
matters that required his attention. Then she stopped.

"I do not want to tire you with too much all at
once. You know what Dr. Jenkins said about how
careful you were to be not to over-excite yourself, and
I think perhaps we should do the improvements very,
very slowly."

"If you feel that would be wise."

"Yes indeed," she said quickly.

"We will talk about it, but I promise I will not
over-tire myself. But first of all, before I worry about
anything else, I must worry about you."

"Why me?" Purilla enquired.

"Because I am aware that I am a very disappointing bridegroom," the Earl answered, "and I realise
that you may feel defrauded, first for not having had a
large wedding, which every woman wants, and secondly because your bridegroom is somewhat igno-
miniously incapacitated."

Purilla laughed.

"I thought our wedding was very beautiful, and I had no wish to have anyone else there except Nanny and Jason."

"And of course Mercury at the porch."

"I think he understood that something very special was happening," Purilla said, "and he is very impressed with his stable here and the smart horses he has to talk to."

Now she was being a child again, and the Earl felt it was intriguing and rather fascinating how she could switch from being an earnest reformer concerning the troubles and conditions of the labourers to speaking of her own life as if she were living in a fairy-tale.

Apparently she had finished what she had to say, and the Earl said quietly:

"You have mentioned Nanny and Jason, but you have not said there was someone else in the Church that you paricularly wanted to be there."

It took a few seconds before Purilla understood. Then she said:

"I had not ... forgotten ... you."

"I thought perhaps you had."

"No, of course not, but I knew you were not feeling well, and when you looked so ill when we reached here, I was afraid, terribly afraid, that getting married was too much for you and I should have made you wait for at least a week."

This was the opening that the Earl had been waiting for, and he searched amongst his papers until he found a copy of the announcement Mr. Anstruther had sent to a London newspaper.

The Earl had worded it with great care, hoping to make it sound as if it were an announcement written by the editor rather than by himself.

He looked at it now before he handed it to Purilla, saying:

"I want you to read this."

She took it from him and he thought that her eyes were a little apprehensive as she did so, as if she somehow sensed there was a note of mystery in his voice.

She read:

> We have only just learnt of the marriage of the Earl of Rockbrook and Purilla, daughter of the late Colonel Edward Cranford and the late Mrs. Cranford of the Manor House, Little Stanton, Buckinghamshire. The ceremony took place some time ago very quietly owing to family mourning.
>
> The announcement was further delayed owing to injuries incurred by the Earl when out riding, and he is still not fully restored to health.
>
> The Earl and Countess of Rockbrook are now in residence at Rock House in Buckinghamshire, and we offer them our most sincere congratulations and good wishes for their future happiness.

As Purilla read the announcement there was a little frown between her eyes, and she said:

"But we were not married 'some time ago.' "

"I know," the Earl replied, "but I have special reasons for wishing the marriage to appear to have taken place sooner than it did."

There was silence. Then Purilla said:

"You mean . . . you do not wish to tell me why we are having to . . . lie about it?"

" 'Lie' is a harsh word," the Earl said quickly. "I prefer to think of it as an inaccuracy of no particular interest to anyone except ourselves."

"It seems strange, and perhaps it might be . . . unlucky."

"As I have said, it cannot affect anyone but us," the Earl said, "and I have only told you this in case we are questioned."

"Who is likely to do that?"

"No-one I can think of."

"They will know in Little Stanton that it is not true."

"The only person in Little Stanton who knows we have been married is the Vicar," the Earl said.

Purilla did not contradict him, but she was quite certain that somehow, almost as if the information were blown on the wind, everybody would have been aware that when she went to Rock it was as the Earl's wife.

She felt that if the Earl wished to believe that the ceremony in the Church had been an absolute secret, there was no reason for her to disillusion him.

At the same time, she was of course curious as to why he wanted to pretend it had happened some time ago.

Aloud she said:

"Elizabeth knows when we were married."

"You have heard from her?" the Earl enquired.

"Yes. A letter came this morning, She is excited and of course delighted that I am a bride, as she will be in two weeks' time."

She paused before she added:

"I think she would be disappointed if you were not well enough to go to her wedding."

"I shall certainly be well enough," he replied. "Actually, I feel well enough already to ride or do anything else I want to do."

"No, no!" Purilla said quickly. "You promised Dr. Jenkins you would not do anything for a week except walk about and sit in the sun. You cannot go back on your promise."

"Jenkins is an old woman," the Earl declared, "and you and Nanny are mollycoddling me to the point where I shall get so fat and lazy that I shall never be able to do anything strenuous again."

"I think that is very unlikely," Purilla said with a smile, "but you must still keep your promise. I could not bear you to be ill."

The Earl was remembering that Dr. Jenkins had been very insistent.

"What you have had is a warning, My Lord," he had said, "and you must therefore heed it and take things really easy for at least a week. That means no riding, no bumping about in a carriage, and no love-making."

He misunderstood the frown between the Earl's

eyes, who was resenting anyone interfering in his private affairs.

"It may seem hard on you, but you have had a very quick marriage, and since you are not fit, it would be a mistake to start off on the wrong foot, so to speak. Give yourself time, and if you take my advice you will, having dispensed with an engagement, do your wooing at your leisure."

The Earl did not reply, and as if he felt he had perhaps gone too far in what he had said, Dr. Jenkins hastily made his farewells.

The Earl was well aware that what he had advised was sheer common sense, and although he hated to admit it, he knew that in arranging his marriage to take place so hastily, he had not considered his bride's feelings as a woman.

The more he saw of Purilla, the more he realised that she did not fit into the image he had planned of a quiet, complacent, grateful wife with simple country tastes and with a somewhat limited intelligence.

The Earl knew now that she was curious and puzzled by his deception over the date of their wedding.

However, it was impossible for him to tell her the truth, and he would just have to think of some reasonable explanation.

She was still staring down at the paper in her hands and after a moment she said:

"If people ask me ... when we were married, you will ... expect me to ... lie."

"People will not ask us the date," the Earl replied. "They are much more likely to enquire where, and then of course you can tell the truth. One reason, which I am sure you will understand, is that most people in the Social World will think it strange that we did not invite my many relatives or ask you to meet them before we were actually married."

"I forgot you would have a lot of relatives, while I have none," Purilla said.

"I regret to tell you they are innumerable," the Earl answered, "and doubtless you will meet them all in good time. But as they did not pay much attention

to me these past years, I really have no wish to
entertain them so quickly after my uncle's death."

"But will they not think it very strange that you
got married without telling them?"

"They knew I had no expectation of inheriting,"
the Earl replied, "and they will therefore suppose that
I had no wish to wait for a long time to be married
simply because I was in mourning. It would obviously
be easier for me to be married very quietly and have
you meet the family later."

He congratulated himself that this sounded quite
plausible and he thought Purilla accepted it. Then she
said:

"I will of course do ... anything to ... help you,
and I am glad we can be ... alone until you feel ...
better."

It was what the Earl wanted to hear her say, and
he put out his hand towards her.

"You are very understanding, Purilla," he said,
"and I am very grateful. Let us hope people do leave
us alone so that we can get to know each other."

"I feel I know you already and have done for
years and years ... perhaps centuries in another life."

The Earl looked surprised, and she explained:

"When I first saw you I somehow felt that I had
seen you somewhere. It was Richard who told me
how people in India believe in the Wheel of Rebirth,
and I have often thought about it and wondered if I
should ever meet anyone who had been with me in
another life."

"So you think we have known each other before?"

"I am sure of it."

"Then it is something I must believe as well," he
said. "I cannot have you isolated, even in your
thoughts."

He saw that this pleased her, and he felt her
fingers move in his.

He raised her hand to his lips and kissed it, and
now for the first time since he had known her he felt a
tremor run through her at his touch and knew he
excited her.

"You are a very lovely, sweet person, Purilla," he said, "and may I say that even if we have been acquainted for a million years, there is still a great deal more I want to know about you."

He thought that her blue eyes seemed to fill her whole face. Then she said:

"I am so lucky ... so very lucky to have ... found you. I know now that what I have been seeking has been you ... but I was not really sure of it until you ... asked me to ... marry you."

The Earl told himself that he should reciprocate by telling her that likewise he had been seeking her, but he had an uncomfortable feeling that unless it was true, which it was not, Purilla would sense that he was only paying her "lip service."

Aloud he said:

"You must tell me about this belief of yours. Of course when I was in India I knew it was part of the Buddhist and Hindu religions, but I never had time to study it. I was too busy training the troops and fighting rebellious tribesmen."

"Richard said that India was very, very beautiful."

"Very beauiful," the Earl agreed. "At the same time, I think nothing could be lovelier than our surroundings here at this moment."

Purilla released his hand and rose as he had done to walk to the door of the Orangery and look out into the garden.

As she moved, the Earl thought how her new gown accentuated the soft curves of her body and how gracefully she walked.

As he looked at her he told himself that with the sunshine on her fair hair, it would be difficult to find anyone lovelier or in fact with the sensitive delicacy of a portrait by Sir Joshua Reynolds.

'I am lucky,' he thought to himself, 'more lucky than I can possibly express.'

It suddenly struck him that it might have been Louise standing there instead of Purilla, and he shuddered at the thought.

He had a sudden feeling that Purilla was like an angel guarding and protecting him from the dangers that had encroached far too near for comfort.

Then he knew that she did in fact exemplify the lily with which he had first identified her; a lily which looked at him with blue eyes filled with a love that was not physical but spiritual.

The Earl suddenly reached out his hands.

"Come here, Purilla!" he said.

She turned at his command and came towards him.

He took both her hands in his.

"Listen to me," he said. "I want to tell you how beautiful you are and how much I admire the way you are behaving in what I know are very difficult circumstances."

Her fingers tightened on his and she looked at him in a puzzled fashion.

"I am sure this is not the sort of marriage you imagined in your dreams," he went on, "but I want you to know how proud of you I am and how much I enjoy having you here with me at Rock."

It was what he thought he ought to say. At the same time, the words were genuinely sincere and he knew they meant a great deal to Purilla.

Yet her eyes were looking into his and he felt she was searching deep down inside him, looking for something, searching for the Golden Fleece which was an indivisible part of the marriage she wanted.

After a moment he raised one of her hands to his lips, then the other.

Her skin was very soft and he thought as his mouth lingered for a moment that if he kissed her lips they would also be soft, sweet, and innocent.

Then he told himself that it was too soon and the Doctor was right: he should wait and not rush things.

He raised his head to look at Purilla and saw that there was a flush on her cheeks and her lips were parted as if she found it difficult to breathe.

He knew that his kissing her hand had aroused feelings she had never known before, and once again

the Earl wanted to kiss her lips and hold her against
him.

Then she released her hands from his, and in a
shy little voice which was different from usual she
said:

"I ... I must go and ... find Jason. It is ... time I
took him for a ... walk."

She went from the Orangery and the Earl sat
back in his chair, thinking about her.

For the first three days after they were married
Nanny and Bates had made the Earl go to bed early,
and although Purilla had a tray in his bedroom, it was
not the same as tonight, when he was coming downstairs and they were to dine in the small Dining-Room.

Because she was excited at the prospect, she had
asked the gardeners to whom she had already introduced herself if they would decorate the table.

"The flowers are so lovely," she had said flatter-
ingly to the Head Gardener, who had been at Rock
for over thirty-five years, "that I cannot bear to think
they must ever die."

"If they lasted too long, M'Lady, you'd soon 'ave
nowheres to put the fresh 'uns," the old man said with
a chuckle.

"That is true," Purilla agreed, "but every day I
think the arrangements are prettier than the day before, so please make the table very special for His
Lordship. I know he will appreciate it."

The gardener replied that that presented no difficulties, and Purilla was then faced with the problem
of what to wear.

Almost every day new gowns arrived from London, besides bonnets, shawls, pelisses, shoes, gloves,
and the most alluring lace-trimmed underwear she
had ever imagined.

The dressmaker who had called after her arrival
had seemed to understand, without being told, exactly
what was required for the trousseau. But Purilla was
nevertheless overwhelmed at the amount of things
which were sent her, although Nanny and the Earl
seemed to take it as a matter of course.

"It must all have cost an awful lot of money," she

had said in a frightened tone to Nanny that very morning when still more boxes had arrived.

"His Lordship can afford it," Nanny replied, "and you know as well as I do, Miss Purilla, you can hardly go about here in those rags and tags which was all you had to wear at home."

"I was quite happy in them," Purilla replied defensively.

"There's gratitude for you!" Nanny said sharply. "With His Lordship paying a fortune to deck you out as a Lady of Fashion!"

"I do not wish to be a Lady of Fashion," Purilla answered. "I just want him to think that I look attractive."

"He has eyes in his head, I suppose," Nanny said abruptly.

She did not say any more, but Purilla was aware that she thought her marriage was not only unusual but somehow embarrassing.

She knew the old woman well enough to realise that first of all Nanny did not like the haste in which she had been made the Earl's wife, and secondly, the fact that he had not been able to behave as a bridegroom had not escaped her attention.

As he was her patient, she knew it was right and prudent for him to sleep in his own room and treat Purilla almost as if she were his sister rather than his wife.

But another side of her resented the fact that Purilla had not been swept off her feet by an ardent suitor who loved her as she should be loved.

"He will love me . . . eventually," Purilla said to Jason before she went to sleep that night.

He had his basket, but when Nanny was out of the way, he would often jump up on the bed and creep close to Purilla.

"He is so magnificent, so impressive," she went on, "and there must be so many women who have loved him, and perhaps he has loved them . . . but I have nothing to offer him . . . except my heart."

There was a wistful note in her voice which made Jason snuggle a little closer to her.

She put her arms round him, feeling that the warmth and softness of his body was somehow comforting.

"I think he trusts me," she reasoned, "and I think perhaps I can help him with the people on the Estate. He understood what I was trying to tell him about them, but I want him to feel I matter to him more than anything else in the world, more than his title or his money...."

She gave a deep sigh.

"Perhaps it is too much to ask and we are both lucky to be here. I know it is greedy to want more, but, Jason, I want his love, I want it desperately"

She felt the tears come into her eyes, and, holding Jason close against her, she thought of the Earl sleeping in the next room.

There was a communicating-door between them and she knew she had only to open it to see him and hear him.

She wondered what he would think if she asked if she could just sit and talk with him for a little while. Then she told herself it would be a very pushy thing to do.

After all, she was in her nightgown and the Earl had never seen her like that, with her hair hanging over her shoulders. He had never suggested that she should even come and say good-night to him after she was undressed.

"I will wait for him to ... kiss me ... then perhaps he will come to my ... room," she told herself.

But she was not sure of anything except that their marriage was not a real one.

The next day the Earl came downstairs soon after breakfast.

Purilla had been late getting up, and as she came down the stairs he was waiting for her, looking, she thought, so elegant and so athletic that it was difficult to believe he could ever be ill.

"I thought we might visit the stables," he said as she reached him.

"That is what I expected you would wish to do," Purilla answered. "The horses, I am quite certain, know their Master is coming and are watching for you."

"So they too have supernatural powers," the Earl said with a smile.

They had talked about that subject last night at dinner and the Earl had found that it greatly interested her when he told her about the Temples in India and the fakirs and Holy Men.

"Have you any ghosts in this house?" Purilla asked.

"The Curator can show you certain references to them in the documentary records of the house," the Earl replied. "Personally I have never seen one, although my grandmother used to swear she had met a Cavalier walking in the passage, and when she asked what he was doing—he vanished!"

Purilla laughed.

"That must have been very disconcerting. Do you suppose it was a good or a bad omen?"

"I should think it was bad for him," the Earl replied. "He has had to hang about at Rock all these centuries instead of going to the Elysian Fields, or whatever type of Heaven you believe in."

There was a little pause. Then Purilla asked:

"Do you believe in . . . Heaven?"

The way she asked told the Earl that he must answer her seriously.

"To be honest, I am not certain," he replied, "just as I am not certain whether people really have supernatural powers, or whether they are just primitive superstitions which have attracted belief down the ages."

"Perhaps one day you will be able to prove the truth for yourself, which I feel is something we all have to do," Purilla answered.

Then they changed the subject.

Thinking it over later, the Earl was certain that Purilla believed in the supernatural and he would not be in the least surprised if she told him she had seen ghosts at Rock.

As they walked rather slowly, so that the Earl should not unduly exert himself, towards the stables, he thought that Purilla, having been closer to her horse and her dog than to any human being, would naturally expect them to have an instinct and an understanding where she was concerned.

He realised, although she had not told him so, that she could call Jason without actually saying his name aloud.

She would think of him and almost instantly he would come to her.

It struck him as rather extraordinary, but he remembered that a close affinity between men and animals had been established for centuries.

He had not yet seen Purilla with her horse Mercury and this was something he looked forward to.

As they entered the stables there was a whinny from a stall some way from the one they had reached first, and he guessed that the noise was being made by Mercury.

He was not mistaken.

"That 'orse has been making a noise for the last three minutes, M'Lady!" a groom said. "Oi notice each mornin' he seems to know ye're a-comin' afore ye actually arrive."

Purilla smiled and did not contradict the assertion, and the Earl, ignoring his own horses, followed her to the stall where Mercury by this time was making a tremendous commotion.

He stopped the moment Purilla opened the door and at once nuzzled against her. The Earl saw that the horse was actually a well-bred, fine-looking animal, although not quite in the same class as his own horseflesh.

"This is Mercury!" Purilla said unnecessarily.

"So I gathered," the Earl replied. "He was certainly trying to draw attention to himself."

"He has not been trained to do so," Purilla answered. "He loves me and he knows when I am thinking of him."

She thought the Earl looked a little sceptical, but he did not say anything, then after he had patted the horse he said:

"Now that you have greeted Mercury, you must

come and look at my horses or else they will be jealous."

"Can Mercury come with us?"

"Of course, if you want him to," the Earl agreed.

He thought he might have expected that Mercury would follow them like a dog and walk quietly, almost respectfully, behind Purilla and stop as they went into each of the other stalls to inspect the Earl's horses.

They were certainly very fine, and Purilla liked the most spirited and the most difficult ones, which again was what the Earl had expected.

He had not thought of her as an Amazon, but now he knew that it was the love she gave the animals which seemed to make them immediately amenable.

Even those who would not respond to him nuzzled their noses against Purilla and seemed to want her to touch them.

They visited all the horses before she said:

"I think now you should return to the house. You have been walking about for over an hour, and Nanny said you were to have some strengthening soup half-way through the morning."

"I will not allow her to fuss over me much longer!" the Earl said.

"She will do that whether you try to stop her or not," Purilla laughed, "and actually you should be grateful."

He knew that was not the end of the sentence, and he waited until Purilla went on:

"Nanny not only thinks of you as her patient and her charge but is beginning to love you, just as your horses will love you when they know you better. Mercury loves you already."

"I suppose he told you so," the Earl said a little sarcastically.

"When you touch him he quivers in a special type of way, as he does when he is with me," Purilla answered. "When other people pat him it is not the same."

She spoke simply, and the Earl knew it was impossible to laugh at her fancy, even though he thought it was one.

"As you say, I am very lucky," he remarked, "and I presume you are envisaging this affection becoming an ever-widening circle until it embraces the whole Estate?"

"Of course," Purilla replied. "Surely that is what you are aiming for? There is no point in calling it your home if it is not a place of love, where people trust you and know that you care for them."

It flashed through the Earl's mind that most Landlords would think this an absurdly sentimental attitude.

Then he told himself that of course, although it was slightly embarrassing to think about it, Purilla was right.

A home should be founded on love, and those who worked for it either inside or outside must give their hearts as well as their labour if their work was to be worthwhile.

In the hard, somewhat austere life he had lived as a soldier, such thoughts and feelings had never entered his mind.

He knew that his men admired him. They were prepared to follow him, but he had never expected them to have any sentimental feelings for him. He told himself that what Purilla was saying was merely a woman's point of view and something he would agree with politely but would otherwise ignore.

Then he knew that she was right and that Rock, because it meant so much to him and the generations before him, was worth more than "lip service" and paid labour.

He would infuse the right spirit into it, the spirit which animated and sustained the famous Regiments and which evoked a loyalty that was really equivalent to a kind of love.

A man could love his Regiment. For him it could stand for everything that was fine and inspiring and could become so much a part of his life that he was helpless without it.

The Earl had a sudden memory of all the things he had meant, in his new position, to do in London— the place he would occupy at Court, the friends he could now afford to entertain, and the places of amusement he could visit.

Then he knew that Purilla was right. Rock came first. Rock had to be improved, renovated, and modernised.

Then and only then, when it was as perfect as he wanted it to be, would he be free to amuse himself elsewhere.

"That will certainly be a long time ahead," he told himself.

Somehow it was not a depressing thought but a challenge and an invigorating one.

There was a lot to be done, and Purilla had shown him what it was.

Chapter Six

The Earl was feeling so much better that he had
an irresistible impulse to ride.

There were still two days left of the time set by
Dr. Jenkins for him to rest, and although he thought it
was unnecessary, he also felt he could not face a
wordy argument with Nanny, Bates, and of course
Purilla.

He told himself he was fortunate that there were
three people who cared so much for his well-being.

At the same time, he found it irritating to be
mollycoddled after years of the hardship which was
an inevitable part of most soldiers' lives.

However, he busied himself with the plans he
was making for improving conditions on the Estate,
and when he discussed them with Purilla he became
more and more surprised at how much she knew
about the difficulties of the farm-labourers and how
important their troubles were to her.

Sitting in the Library or in one of the magnificent
State-Rooms, in her new gowns she looked so lovely
and at the same time so fragile and fairy-like that it
seemed impossible that anything mundane or commonplace should concern her.

And yet she and the Earl had quite a spirited
argument on what the increase in wages should be

once the threshing-machine was installed, and another concerning the building of cottages for those of his employees who had large families.

"If we make them too attractive, their families will increase out of all proportion," he said.

He spoke more because it amused him to see what she would reply than because he felt very deeply on the subject.

"I have always believed that large families are the happiest," Purilla said.

"Having no experience of them, how would you know?" the Earl enquired.

"I would like to have had a dozen brothers, and when Richard was killed I was left all . . . alone."

There was something so wistful in the way she spoke that the Earl wanted to put his arms round her and prevent her from ever feeling lonely again.

He told himself that he had already decided not to be affectionate but to keep their relationship on a friendly basis until he was well enough to talk of love, which inevitably he had to do, sooner or later.

He was still nervous, although he tried not to admit it to himself, that when he did so she would sense that he did not love her in the idealistic way that she had wanted from the Prince Charming of her dreams.

The Earl told himself cynically that this was something that did not really exist in a hard, material-istic world.

Eventually Purilla would have to face reality and realise what while he would love her in his own way, it could not be the ecstatic rapture for which she longed.

He found himself lying awake at night, wonder-ing how he could prevent himself from disillusioning her.

He told himself that she was so child-like in many ways, especially in her innocence, that he was facing a problem he had never had to face before with any other woman in his life.

He had the feeling that like the lily with whom

he had identified her, it would be easy to besmirch something that was fresh and beautiful and which ideally should never be touched by human hands.

Then he told himself almost roughly that his imagination was running away with him and Purilla after all was only an ordinary young girl—a species of which he had very little experience.

He thought that in the days they had been at Rock they had developed a pleasant intimacy and he often found surprisingly that she read his thoughts before he expressed them.

He too had an instinct for what she was feeling, even though he did not express it in words.

Now when she joined him in the Silver Salon, which, decorated with flowers, looked more feminine and more used than since he had inherited, he told himself that the love he saw in her eyes was becoming more obvious day by day.

"She loves me," he told himself, and knew it was a different love from what he had ever been offered before.

Purilla came to his side and he put out his hand and she slipped hers into it.

"Are you well enough to do something very exciting this afternoon?" she asked.

"I feel well enough for anything," he replied. "As a matter of fact, I was just wishing I could go riding."

"No! It is too soon!" she said quickly. "But I thought perhaps we might explore just a little of the house together. I am finding it very difficult to keep my eyes shut as I promised you I would."

The Earl laughed.

"I am convinced you have cheated a little and peeped from time to time, but of course I will take you on a Grand Tour. I think we should start with the State-Rooms on the Ground Floor."

"That is what I was thinking too," Purilla said, "so that you would not be tired by going upstairs."

"There is so much to see," the Earl said, "that it will be several days before I have introduced you to everything I possess."

Purilla's fingers tightened on his and she gave what he knew was a little skip of excitement.

"Please let us start now," she said. "I cannot tell you how thrilling it will be for me."

She looked so lovely as she spoke, with her eyes shining and her lips parted, that the Earl felt an almost irresistible impulse to kiss her.

He had lain awake last night thinking that he had never kissed a woman who had never been kissed before, and he was sure that Purilla's lips would be very soft and somehow defenceless.

He felt a throb of excitement at the thought of being the teacher in a new and hitherto unexplored territory of love.

Always in the past, sophisticated women who had given themselves to him almost over-eagerly had been as passionate as he was, and it had in fact been a case of two fires blending together into a burning blaze.

But with Purilla the Earl knew it would be very different and he would have to control himself strictly so as not to frighten or shock her; at the same time, he would have to initiate her into the joy of love so that she found with him the happiness she was seeking.

Because he wanted to kiss her, he looked away from her excited little face, which seemed to have a light behind it, and said almost abruptly:

"We will start with the State Drawing-Room, which I have seen open in the past only on very important occasions."

Still holding her hand, they moved towards the door, when it opened and the Butler came into the Salon to announce:

"The Duke of Torrington, M'Lord, and Lady Louise Welwyn."

The Earl stood still with Purilla beside him and he thought that he might have expected his nemesis to catch up with him at an inconvenient moment.

He released Purilla's hand and walked forward.

"This is a surprise, Your Grace!" he remarked.

The Duke inclined his head but did not hold out his hand, and the Earl managed to prevent himself from making the expected gesture of welcome.

He was aware without even looking at her that Lady Louise was staring at him with dark, resentful eyes, and he could not ignore the scowl on the Duke's face that made him look even more formidable than he usually did.

"I wish to speak to you privately, Rockbrook," the Duke said.

The Earl realised that this was to be an uncomfortable interview and was not a social call.

He was about to turn his head to ask Purilla to leave them, but with her usual intuition where he was concerned, she was already moving towards the door.

As she passed through it, the Duke said:

"I consider, Rockbrook, that you have treated my daughter extremely badly and I require an explanation."

There was no doubt that his tone was aggressive and that the hidden threat behind the words was that he intended to make things very awkward.

There was just a moment's hesitation before the Earl said in what he hoped was a surprised voice:

"I am afraid I do not understand, Your Grace. Whatever feelings Lady Louise and I had for each other, I cannot believe that you would have accepted as a suitable son-in-law a penniless Captain who could not afford to live on his pay."

His reply was obviously not what the Duke had expected and there was a distinct pause before he said:

"Are you telling me that you were married before you inherited your uncle's title?"

"My uncle and his son were killed the third week in March."

"But the announcement spoke of 'family mourning.'"

"My wife's only brother was killed in India last November."

Again there was a pause. Then as if the ground had been cut from under his feet, the Duke turned to his daughter.

Now the hostility had left her eyes and she was looking round at the Earl in a very different way.

"Why could you not have waited?" she asked in what was little more than a broken whisper.

The Earl made a gesture with his hands.

"How could I have known, how could I have guessed," he asked, "that both my uncle and his only son would be killed in such an unfortunate, tragic manner?"

There was a pregnant silence.

"In the circumstances," the Duke said at length, "I must apologise for misjudging you."

"Please allow me to offer you some refreshment," the Earl said. "Have you come from London?"

"We are on our way to stay with Sir Francis Dashwood at High Wycombe," the Duke replied.

"I have not seen him for some years," the Earl answered conversationally, "but I hope now that I shall be able to renew the acquaintance."

While he was speaking, Louise had moved down the Salon and seated herself on a sofa near the flower-filled fireplace.

She was looking round, and the Earl was aware how angry and jealous she was now that there was no chance of her being the Chatelaine of Rock as she would have wished to be.

He could understand that once she had realised he was not only a rich man but of importance in the Social World, she had been determined, as she had not been when they had first met, to make him her husband.

The Earl was certain that she had worked assiduously on her father to make him take the course he had.

No man likes to force another into marriage with his daughter, and he wondered how much of the truth Louise had told the Duke about their association at Windsor Castle.

At the same time, his plan had worked exactly as he had hoped it would.

That he had been married when he was of no social importance must completely undermine any objections the Duke could make, while Louise could, if she wished, allot him the role of frustrated lover who saw no chance of ever attaining his desires.

Then, as if she was still suspicious, Louise asked suddenly:

"If you were as poor as you say you were, how could you afford to marry anyone?"

The Earl had anticipated this question and had the answer ready.

"My wife comes from an Army family and is used to managing on very little," he said. "She has a small income of her own and a Manor House not far from here, where we would have lived when I was not with the Regiment."

It all sounded very plausible, and the Duke said:

"Of course, if your wife was a neighbour, you would have known her for many years."

The Earl was not obliged to tell any more lies for the moment because, as if he had anticipated what might be required, the Butler came into the room followed by a footman carrying a tray on which there were glasses and a silver wine-cooler in which reposed an opened bottle of champagne.

The Duke took a glass with obvious relish.

"I must of course drink your health, Rockbrook," he said, "and I hope I may have the pleasure of meeting your wife."

"I am sure she will be honoured to meet you, Your Grace," the Earl replied, "but as she is rather shy, I think perhaps we will wait for another occasion."

The Duke was sophisticated enough to understand that the Earl was telling him that there was no point in Lady Louise and the new Countess being forced into an encounter with each other.

"Yes, yes, you are quite right, and we cannot stay long," the Duke agreed.

He managed, however, to drink several more glasses of champagne and to have reached an effusively benign mood before the Earl escorted them to their carriage and stood waiting on the steps until they drove away.

As Louise held his hand when they said good-bye, there was a look in her eyes which might have made him apprehensive.

It told him all too clearly that her passion for him was not spent, and that having failed to make trouble she would undoubtedly try to inveigle him back into her clutches in a very different manner when they met again.

But as the carriage disappeared down the drive the Earl knew with a feeling of inexpressible relief that she no longer menaced him, and the fear of what had seemed to haunt him for so long had vanished like mist in sunshine.

He was free! Free of Louise and her fiery, unnatural passion! Free of what had been almost a terror of finding himself married to a woman he disliked and despised!

He was smiling as he walked into the Hall.

"Ask Her Ladyship to join me in the Salon," he said to the Butler, then walked back into the flower-filled room to pour himself another glass of champagne.

Before he drank he raised his glass in a silent toast.

"To my future happiness!" he said beneath his breath, and felt as if the room was filled with sunshine.

*　　*　　*

Walking through the shrubberies with Jason at her heels, Purilla was driven by an inexpressible impulse to get away somewhere where she could think.

When she had gone from the Salon, before she had closed the door she had heard the Duke say:

"I consider, Rockbrook, that you have treated my daughter extremely badly and I require an explanation."

The tone in the Duke's voice as well as his words made her heart give a little throb of fear, and she had stood still, holding the door-handle but not closing the door completely.

She heard the Earl's reply and knew that it was the answer to what had puzzled her and compelled her to keep wondering why he had married her and why he had lied about the date on which the wedding had taken place.

Now she understood, and although it seemed to her impossible that he should wish to escape from anybody so beautiful and elegant as Lady Louise, she knew now that their marriage had been his solution to the problem of saving himself. He had not in fact loved her as she had tried to believe he had.

'I was just the lesser of two evils,' she thought as she walked on.

She did not see the purple and white lilac, the syringa whose fragrance filled the air, or the almond blossom as fragile and delicate as the flush on her young cheeks.

'How could I have known... how could I have guessed that was the only reason he wanted me?' she wondered to herself.

She felt as if he had swept her along on the wave of his determination. It had been impossible to withstand it even while her instinct had told her that however reasonable he made it appear, it was not the right way to be married.

"But how can I help loving him?" she asked aloud.

Jason looked up at her, wondering at the pain in her voice.

"He is so handsome, so magnificent," she said, "and I love him more every time I see him, but that does not excuse his means of eluding the lovely Lady Louise."

She knew now that she had always half-suspected there was some secret explanation, apart from his injuries, for the Earl being in such desperate haste for them to be married.

It was only because she loved him so desperately that she had allowed herself to pretend that it was because he wanted her and that she could not be at Rock unmarried, even with Nanny, without a Chaperone.

Of course, if he had really wanted one, he could have found a Chaperone amongst his many relatives, or alternatively, as she was so unimportant, surely it would not have mattered whether she was chaperoned or not.

Instead, he had thought up this strange and what now seemed fantastic means of saving himself from being pressured into marriage with the Duke's daughter, although why he should not want to marry her Purilla could not understand.

However, she realised that the Earl's explanation that a penniless soldier was not likely to commend himself to the Duke was extremely clever.

Purilla was well aware that in an expensive Regiment like the Grenadier Guards, every officer had to have private means, since it was impossible for him to exist on his pay.

She suspected, because her father had often discussed with her the expenses of the different Regiments, that the Earl must have had a small income which had been just sufficient for his needs if he was very economical, and it would have been impossible in the circumstances for him to marry a wife·who had no money of her own.

"If he had loved Lady Louise, as she obviously loves him," Purilla reasoned, "they would have managed somehow and perhaps he would even have left the Regiment."

When she saw Lady Louise come into the Salon, Purilla had thought she was so beautiful, so alluring, that her first feeling had been one of jealousy. She thought that beside such a vision she would appear very ordinary and unattractive.

Now, although it seemed incredible, the Earl had preferred to be married to her rather than to Lady Louise, and she supposed that in a way it was a compliment.

But it was not enough.

She wanted love, the love she had been trying to pretend to herself he had for her, the love that she knew in her heart was essential to a marriage if it was to be complete and happy.

"How can I bear it? How can I live with him knowing that he never wanted me as a ... person, but only as a ... raft or a life-buoy to save him from a ... worse fate?"

She reached the end of the shrubberies and started to climb through the trees of a small wood which lay beyond them.

Now Jason ran ahead, searching for rabbits amongst the undergrowth, while Purilla walked blindly, not seeing her surroundings but only the Earl's handsome face.

She felt he had been much kinder and in a way more affectionate these last few days, and she thought it was because he was feeling better in health and also because when they talked together they seemed to have so many things in common.

But she was afraid that now even their companionship would no longer be of any interest to him.

"You expected the Duke to challenge your behaviour," she told the Earl in her mind, "and that is why you pretended to be married before you had inherited."

She had always been aware, if she was honest, that there was a shadow between them, or perhaps it was a gulf. Now, as the Duke believed the Earl, he was ... free.

Free, except that he was ... married to someone he did not ... love.

Purilla cried out at the misery of it, and because she felt that only by walking could she try to sort things out in her own mind, she walked on.

She and Jason came from the shelter of the trees to some rough, unfarmed grassland. There were clumps of low bushes and there was an incline which was almost a small hill in front of them.

Jason ran ahead, then almost at his feet a small rabbit dashed from the shelter of a bush and rushed wildly away, its white tail bobbing behind it.

Jason gave a bark of excitement, and, seeing what had happened, Purilla opened her lips to call him back.

Even as she did so, she saw him disappear into

the hill ahead of her and wondered vaguely where he had gone.

It took her a little time to walk over the rough ground until, as she neared the point where Jason had disappeared, she saw what looked like the opening of a cave.

There were large lumps of what she recognised as white chalk lying at the entrance, and she suddenly realised that it was one of the chalk-mines that were to be found in many parts of Buckinghamshire.

She had heard so often of the chalk-caves of West Wycombe which had been used by the wicked Sir Francis Dashwood in the Eighteenth Century for the most immoral and disreputable orgies.

There were also several other caves near Little Stanton in which a certain amount of mining had been done by farmers, and she thought that this one had obviously not been worked for a long time.

As she reached the darkness of the entrance she could hear Jason barking inside and she guessed he had either got the rabbit cornered or else it had disappeared down a hole and he could no longer reach it.

"Jason" she called. "Jason!"

The dog did not respond, and as he was usually very obedient she suspected that because his bark echoed and re-echoed in the cave, it was impossible for him to hear anything but his own noise.

She moved farther into the cave.

"Jason!" she called again, but he still went on barking.

The cave had been worked so that it was about four feet wide and over six feet high. The ground was thick with powdered chalk and she thought her shoes would be in a mess, which would annoy Nanny. But there was nothing she could do but try to persuade Jason to leave the rabbit and come out.

"Jason!" she called again, and this time he ceased barking and she knew he must have heard her.

"Jason! Jason!"

She moved still farther on down the passage and now she thought she heard him coming towards her.

Even as he did so, there was a sudden rumble, followed by a crash, then several further crashes, one after another, and she was suddenly in darkness.

It was not difficult to know what had happened.

The entrance to the cave had fallen in, and as Jason reached her side she bent down to put her arms round him, knowing they were trapped.

* * *

The Earl poured himself another glass of champagne but did not drink it.

Instead, carrying it in his hand, he walked towards the window to look out into the garden.

The sunshine was turning the lake to gold and he thought the shrubs and fruit trees had never looked more beautiful.

He knew it was because they were his that he felt a warmth seeping through his body and bringing him not only the joy of possession but a sense of peace he had not known for a long time.

He had a sudden feeling that he wanted to share this new emotion with Purilla, and even as he thought about her, he heard someone come into the room and turned with a smile on his lips.

But it was only the Butler.

"Her Ladyship's not upstairs, M'Lord," he said. "Nurse says she thinks she's gone for a walk."

The Earl frowned.

"Are you sure?" he asked. "Did anyone see Her Ladyship go?"

"I don't think so, M'Lord, but I'll find out."

The Earl put down his glass and walked back to the fireplace to stand on the hearth-rug, thinking.

Purilla had been looking forward to seeing the house with him, but he was sure that if she had gone for a walk it was because she was perturbed and, as he knew she had done in the past, had gone away to think.

That meant that she had been upset by the Duke and Lady Louise, especially the latter.

The Earl was aware that anyone who was in love with him would obviously be jealous of another woman.

Then he realised it was quite possible that Purilla had heard the Duke's peremptory command for an explanation.

"Dammit!" the Earl said to himself. "Why should they come here upsetting things?"

He knew as he spoke that this was what he had anticipated would happen sooner or later, and perhaps it was best to get it over with.

It seemed to him he waited for a very long time before the Butler returned.

"I am unable to find Her Ladyship," he said, "and although none of the household staff saw her leave, one of the gardeners saw her walking across the shrubberies with her dog."

"Thank you," the Earl said. "I expect she will not be long."

He was speaking to himself rather than to the servant, and when he was alone he walked once again to the window, but now he did not see the sun on the lake or the flowers and shrubs.

Instead he was worrying about Purilla, and he had an uncomfortable feeling that she was unhappy and perhaps suffering because she loved him.

"I should have told her the truth when I showed her the notice I inserted in the newspapers," he told himself.

It would have been far better if he had given her his explanation instead of her being upset and misled by the Duke's attitude.

But it was too late now to undo what had already been done. All he could hope was that she would not be long and he could set things right the moment she returned.

* * *

Jason was trembling, and Purilla, holding him close in her arms, waited for more crashes of falling chalk, but there was only a silence in which, because she was frightened, she thought she could hear her own heart beating.

"It is no use just waiting for help, Jason," she said. "We have to try to get out of here."

At first she had felt she was in jet-black darkness, but now there was a faint light on the ground and as she went towards it she realised that one huge boulder had fallen so as to leave an opening through which a little light and fresh air could percolate.

The same applied to other places in the fallen chalk, but she estimated that there was now a large number of boulders firmly embedded one with the other between herself and the entrance.

She knew that if she tried to move any of them, more might collapse on her head.

She stood a long time staring at it helplessly while Jason, as if he realised the predicament they were in, whimpered beside her.

"What shall we do, Jason? What shall we do?" Purcilla asked.

She sat down on the ground and put her arms round him again, feeling that somehow his warmth and the fact that he licked at her face lovingly was some comfort.

It was frightening to realise that no-one knew where she was.

Because she had been so upset she had walked out of the house without even putting on her bonnet.

Fortunately her silk gown was lined and the sleeves reached nearly to her wrists, but she knew that it was much colder in the cave than it was outside and soon she would be very cold indeed, especially when the sun went down.

She felt with a sudden panic that no-one would think of looking for her here and that perhaps she and Jason would die of cold and hunger and the Earl would never know what had happened.

That she would never see him again made her feel frantic and she wanted to scream for help.

But she knew even as she opened her lips that it would be hopeless.

She had seen no-one since the moment she had left the garden, and she was aware that the rough ground over which she had walked was not farmed, nor were there likely to be any labourers working on this part of the Estate.

"We must do something, Jason," she said desperately, "we must!"

He snuggled a little closer to her as if the fear in her voice affected him.

"We cannot die here ... we cannot!" Purilla said. "And if I do, perhaps Lady Louise will ... insist on the Earl ... marrying her."

The idea seemed even more horrifying than her own predicament, and she knew it was quite true. The moment her death was announced, Lady Louise and her formidable father would be seeking the Earl again and forcing him into the marriage he had managed to avoid by marrying her.

"I must save him ... I must save him!" Purilla told herself, and knew she could do that only by saving herself.

She sat and stared at the fallen chalk in front of her as if by sheer will-power she could magic it away.

Then it struck her that the only thing she had left was the power of thought.

She had not told the Earl, because she had thought he would not understand, but she had plied her brother with questions when he was on leave from India about the powers of the fakirs and how they did magic tricks for which no-one could find an explanation.

"A lot of them use hypnotism," Richard had said, "but they undoubtedly also have a method of mental communication."

"What do they do?" Purilla had asked eagerly.

"It is difficult to explain," Richard answered, "but they can project their thoughts over a long distance."

Purilla waited and he continued:

"There was a sepoy in my Company who came to me and said that his father was dead and asked for leave of absence. As I knew that his father lived nearly three hundred miles away, I asked him how he had heard of the old man's death.

" 'He die last night, Captain Sahib.'

" 'Last night!' I exclaimed. 'But it is impossible for you to know that.'

" 'I was told, Captain Sahib, by my brother and sisters.' "

"What did you do?" Purilla asked.

"Of course I refused to let him go on such an obviously false pretext," Richard replied. "Then two weeks later I learnt that his father had indeed died at exactly the time he had said!"

Purilla told herself now that it was telepathy of some sort, and she thought that unless she was prepared to die in the dark cave, her only chance of survival was to try to communicate with the Earl.

She knew that often when they were together she had been able to read his thoughts and at times he appeared to know what she was thinking even before she told him.

"I must reach him!" she said aloud.

Shutting her eyes, she concentrated the love she had for him in her heart and her whole will on trying to make him aware of what had happened.

*   *   *

An hour later the Earl was walking restlessly up and down the Salon.

He had been out to the Hall three or four times to ask the footmen if there was any sign of Her Ladyship.

Now in some way he could not understand he was growing increasingly anxious.

His common sense told him that she had not been away for very long, and if she was upset by what she had overheard she might stay out, as she had when they were at the Manor, until quite late in the evening.

Then he felt almost as if he could hear her call him.

'I am imagining things,' he thought. 'It is not likely she will come to any harm in the grounds.'

Then insidiously he had a presentiment of danger.

He tried to shrug it away—to convince himself it was just his imagination—but it persisted until it was impossible to put it out of his mind and he knew he had to act.

It seemed then as if he could almost see Purilla's face lifted to his, her blue eyes beseeching him, her lips moving as if she tried to tell him something.

"Dammit all, she is in danger—I know it!" he said aloud.

He pulled the bell and a footman came running.

A quarter-of-an-hour later the Earl was in the saddle, with three grooms also mounted on horses, moving away from the front of the house.

"Boyd and I will go through the shrubberies," the Earl said. "One of you go west of the wood in case Her Ladyship returns back that way, and the other ride through the orchard and cover the east side."

The grooms understood and trotted off, while the Earl, followed by Boyd, his chief groom, rode down the small path that wound between the flowering shrubs and out into the wood behind it.

It seemed to the Earl as he went that his feeling that Purilla was calling him intensified, and now he felt almost frantically that he must reach her, and if he did not do so, he might lose her altogether.

The idea was not based on logic but on some prompting that seemed to arise in his mind.

He had the idea that she was praying and it made him quicken the pace of his horse as he rode, looking to right and left for any sign of Purilla's white gown between the tree-trunks.

But there was only the flutter of pigeons overhead, and when they reached the end of the wood he saw that the sun was sinking and he had a sudden agonising fear that he would not find Purilla before it was dark.

As the trees thinned away at the edge of a field, he drew his horse to a standstill.

"Would Her Ladyship have come as far as this, Boyd?" he asked, feeling that he must speak to somebody, if only to assuage his fears.

"It'd be quite a step, M'Lord," the groom replied, "but if 'er Ladyship was intent on a long walk, 'er might 'ave gone over the chalk-hill ahead of us."

"We will go and look," the Earl said.

He rode over the rough ground and up onto the top of the hill which faced them.

On the other side of it were undulating hillocks for a short distance, then the land plunged down towards a valley through which a stream twisted and turned, until it vanished into the blue horizon.

It was very lovely, but the Earl was concerned only with searching for one small figure, and when there was no sign of anyone he said in a voice that held a note of despair:

"What shall we do now, Boyd? Do you think the others may have found her?"

"If they 'ave, M'Lord, Oi've told 'em to blow the 'unting 'orn which both of them carries."

"That was intelligent of you," the Earl remarked.

He sat listening, hoping against hope that he would hear the sound of a horn coming from one side of the wood or the other.

Then as he lifted his reins preparatory to moving away, Boyd suddenly held up his hand.

"Oi thinks Oi 'ears somethin', M'Lord."

The Earl was still.

"I hear nothing," he said.

Then the groom exclaimed:

"There 'tis again, M'Lord! 'Tis a dog barking! P'raps 'er Ladyship's!"

*   *   *

It had grown very cold in the cave and Purilla knew too that the moisture from the chalk had soaked through her gown to her bare skin.

Because it made her shiver, she ceased to lean

back against the wall and sat bolt upright, still holding Jason closely against her, knowing that he was
frightened in the dark and also perhaps because her
own fears communicated themselves to him.

She had thought and prayed for the Earl until it
seemed as if her whole being went out to him. It was
almost as if she became disembodied and could send
him not only her thoughts but her heart and her
soul.

Her prayers were so intense, so vivid, that she
felt as if she must reach him and she had the feeling
that she had done so and in return he was thinking of
her.

"I love him," she told herself. "I have nothing to
send him but my love. But surely love ... even if it is
not reciprocated, is stronger than ... anything else in
the ... world."

She loved the Earl with her whole being, and
whatever he thought about her, nothing could change
the fact that she felt as if every breath she drew had
become a part of him, and she herself was his completely, whether he wanted her or not.

Now she reached out towards him until she flew
through the air between them and she was in his arms
and his heart was beating against hers.

She was lost in what was a dream, so that she
started quite violently when unexpectedly Jason
barked.

He gave the sharp shrill bark which Nanny dep-
recated and which had made her insist on his being
sent to the stables when the Earl was ill.

It was a bark, Purilla knew, that was not one of
joy or excitement but of warning that there was
someone about.

"What is it, Jason?" she asked. "What do you
hear?"

She could not see him, but she felt he had his
head on one side as if he was listening. He moved a
little away from her so that she was half-afraid he too
would vanish in the darkness and she would be left
alone.

Then he barked again, sharply and noisily, and

moved forward to scratch at the barrier ahead of them.

"What is it?" Purilla asked. "Oh, Jason, perhaps they have found us!"

She tried to shout for help, but her voice was choked in her throat by tears.

Chapter Seven

Purilla put up her hands in protest.

"No, no, I cannot drink one spoonful more."

"It'll keep away the chill, Miss Purilla, " Nanny said firmly. "Heaven knows, you were a frozen icicle when you got back."

Purilla gave a weak little laugh.

"I should certainly have been that if I had had to stay there all night."

She saw Nanny shudder and she knew that she herself had been desperately afraid until, like a miracle, she had heard the Earl's voice.

"Are you there, Purilla?" he had shouted above the noise of Jason's barking.

"I am here ... I am ... here!" she managed to gasp, weakly at first because of her fears, then louder because she was afraid he would not hear her.

"You are not hurt?"

She thought there was real concern in his voice and it was the loveliest sound she had ever heard!

He minded! He really minded that she might have been crushed by the falling chalk.

"No ... I am all ... right," she managed to answer.

"We will get you out."

She could hear him speaking to somebody but

119

she did not care who it was or what he was saying. She only knew with an inexpressible relief that her prayers had brought him to the rescue and she and Jason were not going to die of cold.

Then she started as the shrill note of a hunting-horn blared out.

She could not understand why it was being blown, but she felt it must have something to do with the Earl having found her.

Then she could hear him talking near the opening, obviously inspecting the fallen chalk and discussing how they should move it.

Jason wanted to go on barking but now with excitement, as if he knew that the arrival of the Earl meant they would soon be released from their dark prison.

Because Purilla thought it might annoy them, she held him close in her arms to prevent him from making so much noise.

"We have to be patient," she said to him, "and wait until they can find some way of getting us out."

It actually took a long time.

She heard the voices of two other men and guessed, because she also heard the jingle of bridles, that they had ridden to join the Earl.

There was quite a long consultation before she realised they were trying to move the boulders at the bottom of the pile.

She thought this was a strange thing to do, before she gathered that they were attempting to prop the pile from underneath with large pieces of wood which they must have collected from amongst the trees.

She then understood that the Earl was afraid that further falls of the chalk might not only make her escape more difficult but might fall on her and Jason and injure them.

"He is so clever," she told herself.

She felt her love surging out towards him like a wave from the sea.

Then she remembered that he should not be riding since he had been told to rest for another two days, and she was sure that the reason he had ridden there was that in his mind he had heard her cry for help and had sensed the danger she was in.

Even though she was growing colder every minute, she felt a thrill of excitement to guess that the transmission of thought, which Richard had told her the Indians used, had worked between herself and the Earl.

'It is because I love him,' she thought, knowing it proved what she had always believed, that love is the strongest and the most vital vibration in the whole Universe.

She would now find out what the Earl felt and whether he was aware that she was praying for him with her whole heart, beseeching him to save her.

Then she remembered that he did not love her and therefore it would be embarrassing to tell him of her love for him.

'He must never know what I feel,' she decided.

Perhaps it would be better if he did not learn that she had overheard what the Duke had said and therefore now realised why he had married her.

She felt as if the cold of her body deepened until it touched her heart.

"I love him! I love him!" she whispered as she listened to his voice outside.

But there was no reason to think that anything was really changed between them.

Although he had come to save her, she was still of use to him only in that she had saved him from having to marry Lady Louise.

"How could he have wanted an unimportant country girl for his wife," Purilla questioned, "rather than someone beautiful, sophisticated, and the daughter of a Duke?"

It was a question for which she had no answer.

She knew only that the barrier which she had sensed existing between herself and the Earl was still there and there was no way that she could bridge it.

The three grooms had moved the huge boulder that lay at the bottom of the entrance and it was now in an upright position, supported by some stout pieces of wood.

In doing this they had dislodged some small lumps of chalk, but while the Earl watched anxiously, the roof appeared to be remaining firm and he thought that if they were careful there would be no more falls.

By now there was an opening about a foot wide, and as Purilla saw more daylight coming into the passage, she understood what they were trying to do.

She watched in silence, holding Jason in her arms, and now the Earl asked:

"You are all right, Purilla?"

"Yes."

"Can you see if Jason can squeeze through the hole we have made?"

"Yes, of course," Purilla answered. "He has already been struggling to try to do so."

"Then let him go!" the Earl ordered.

Purilla took her arms from round Jason and he did not need to be told to run through the hole ahead of him into the light outside.

He managed it easily, and as she heard him barking excitedly she knew that he was jumping up at the Earl, delighted at being free.

Purilla watched the hole and when they had made it just a little larger she said:

"I think I could get through it now."

"Are you sure?" the Earl asked from the other side. "You must be careful. If you are rough, the chalk might fall in and hurt you."

"I will be very careful," Purilla promised.

She thought it fortunate that she was so slim.

At the same time, as she put first her head and then her shoulders into the hole, she was afraid that if she pushed too hard she might dislodge the wood and the whole weight of the chalk-boulders would collapse on her back.

She had turned her face down so that none of the chalk would fall on it, and then she felt the Earl's hands under her arms, pulling her very gently until first her hips and then her legs were free.

He pulled her up onto her feet and put his arms round her.

She could hardly believe it was true that she had escaped, and because she was afraid she was going to burst into tears, she hid her face against his shoulder.

His arms were very strong and comforting as he said quietly:

"It is all right, you are safe and now I can take you home."

"You . . . came!" she whispered. "I tried to . . . tell you what had . . . happened."

Her voice was so low and incoherent that she thought he had not heard, for he exclaimed:

"Your gown is wet and you must be very cold."

He took his arms from her, and as she tried to find a handkerchief to wipe her eyes, she realised that he was taking off his coat.

"N-no . . . please!" she protested. "I shall be . . . all right."

He paid no attention but put his coat round her shoulders.

Then she heard him say to the head groom:

"I will carry Her Ladyship on my saddle. Give me your coat to make it more comfortable."

"No . . . no!" Purilla said hastily, as the man obeyed.

"Leave everything to me," the Earl said, and she felt there was nothing further she could say.

The head groom's coat and another from one of the other grooms were laid on the front of the Earl's saddle. Then when he was mounted they lifted Purilla up in front of him.

Since it was his left shoulder which had been injured, the Earl put his right arm round her, holding the reins with his left hand.

She was so worried about him that she wanted to say that it would be quite easy for her to ride one of the other horses.

But she knew that she was in fact so cold that she would find it difficult to hold the reins and keep herself in the saddle without a pommell.

'It is not very ... far,' she thought reassuringly.

At the same time, she knew that the Earl should not be taking any risks with his damaged collarbone.

It was, however, impossible to argue with him, and when he had everything arranged so that she was actually very comfortable on the improvised front of his saddle, they set off, moving slowly.

One groom was sent ahead to warn the household that they were coming, while the other two followed behind, with Jason excitedly running beside them.

It was so wonderful to be close to the Earl, to feel his arms round her, and to know that she was no longer in a prison, and Purilla could only say a prayer of thankfulness secretly in her heart.

"Thank You, God ... thank You ... thank You for saving me, and please let the Earl be ... glad.'

It only took them ten minutes to ride back to the house, to find Nanny fussing over her and scolding her at the same time.

There was a hot bath in which she could soak away the cold that seemed to have seeped into her very bones, and a warm bed, besides hot soup which Nanny insisted on feeding her as if she were a baby.

"No more, Nanny, please ... no more," Purilla pleaded.

"There's a dinner for you in a moment," Nanny replied, "and you will eat sensibly. What you wants is food after an experience like that."

"I want to have dinner with His Lordship."

"His Lordship's dining in his own room and Mr. Bates has insisted on his having a hot bath in case he should be stiff after not having ridden for so long."

"His Lordship will hate being an invalid again."

"If he takes risks with himself he must take the consequences," Nanny replied, "and you'll be lucky if you escape pneumonia, with nothing under that thin gown!"

"I am warm now," Purilla answered, "and instead of grumbling you should be thankful that I was not left there all night."

Nanny made an exclamation that was almost a cry of horror.

Dinner arrived and Purilla ate the delicious dishes provided, even while she missed being with the Earl.

She wanted to be with him, to hear him talk, and to watch the expression in his eyes. Most of all, if she was honest, she wanted to know if he was really glad that he had been able to rescue her.

When she had finished and Nanny was taking the tray away she asked:

"Will His Lorship be coming to see me?"

"I expect so," Nanny replied. "I'm going downstairs now to have my own supper. Is there anything more you want?"

"No, nothing," Purilla replied.

Nanny looked round the bedroom as if she thought she must have forgotten something, but everything was in its place. The curtains were drawn over the long windows and the candles were lit on the dressing-table by the bed.

Oil-lamps were used downstairs, except in the great crystal chandeliers, but the bedrooms were lit by candles, which Purilla thought made the rooms look beautiful and very romantic.

They had already discussed whether the Earl should put in gas-lighting.

"It seems a pity to change anything," Purilla had said.

"If we are to move with the times on the Estate," the Earl had replied with a smile, "I think we must also do so in the house."

"It is so lovely as it is."

"We will not be in a hurry," the Earl had replied. "We will listen to the experts before we make a decision."

Purilla had thought her bedroom, with its painted ceiling and gilded cupids flying on the canopy over her bed, was perfect as it was.

But she was concerned at the moment with looking at the communicating-door which had never been opened since she had come to Rock.

She did not know why, but she felt that tonight, after what had happened, the Earl might come from his bedroom into hers through that special door.

And yet she told herself despairingly that now that he knew she was back at home, he might no longer be interested in her.

Then as she lay back on her pillows, looking at the door, she saw the gold handle being turned and felt her heart leap.

The door opened and the Earl was there.

She had expected, stupidly, that even when he dined alone he would be in evening-dress.

Instead he was wearing the long blue velvet robe which he had worn when he was at the Manor and had first been allowed to get up and sit in the sunshine in the bedroom window, before he was strong enough to do anything else.

Because Purilla was so thrilled to see him, his face seemed to swim in front of her eyes and it was hard to focus on him clearly.

He shut the communicating-door quietly behind him, locked the one into the passage, and walked slowly towards the bed.

She sat up very straight, clenching her fingers together, her fair hair falling over her shoulders, her blue eyes very large in her small face.

The Earl came nearer, and now everything she had meant to ask him seemed to fly out of her mind, and instead she said:

"You ... came when I ... called you. I was so ... afraid you might not ... hear me ... but you ... came! How did you ... know I was in ... danger?"

The Earl smiled and stood beside the bed, looking down at her.

The candlelight seemed to make her head shimmer with gold and he thought there was a light behind her eyes that came from her heart—her heart, which he realised she had sent out towards him and which had told him so clearly that she needed him.

He did not answer for a moment. Then he said:

"I think, Purilla, as we both have a lot to tell each other and a great deal to talk about, I should, if I am to obey the Doctor, Nanny, and Bates, rest as you are doing."

For a moment Purilla did not understand what he meant. Then she said quickly:

"Y-yes ... of course you must ... you should not have been riding ... I realise that."

"I have come to no harm," the Earl said, "but I am sure it would be sensible not to take any further chances."

He walked round to the other side of the bed as he spoke, took off his robe, threw it on a chair, and, pulling back the lace-edged sheets, got into bed.

For a moment Purilla could hardly believe what was happening. Then as the colour rose in her cheeks, she felt her heart begin to thump frantically in her breast.

The Earl lay back against the pillows and said quietly:

"That is better! Now I shall not have to listen to Bates scolding me as I am sure Nanny scolded you."

Purilla managed to give a little laugh.

"She is quite ... certain I shall die of ... pneumonia and that you will be crippled from doing too much too ... soon."

"I am tired of their croaking," the Earl said. "Let us talk about ourselves. I want to say, Purilla, that if I had not found you by now I should have been absolutely desperate with anxiety as to what had happened."

"Did you ... really ... worry?" Purilla whispered.

It was a question she had not meant to ask, but somehow it came to her lips before she could prevent it.

"I will answer that in a moment," the Earl replied, "but first I want you to tell me why you went for a walk when you knew we had planned to explore the house together."

She turned her face away from him, and he thought her small straight nose and her soft lips silhouetted against the candlelight were the loveliest things he had ever seen.

Because she could not find words in which to reply, he said after a moment:

"I think perhaps you heard what the Duke said to me."

"I . . . I did not . . . mean to eavesdrop," Purilla stammered.

"You heard what I realised afterwards I should have told you myself, and now rather belatedly I will explain."

"There is . . . no need," Purilla said. "I . . . wondered why you . . . wanted to marry me so quickly . . . and I know . . . now it was . . . because you did not wish to . . . marry Lady Louise."

Her words seemed to fall over one another. Then before the Earl could reply she said:

"I . . . I cannot understand why you did not wish her to be your . . . wife. She is so . . . beautiful and lives in the same world you do . . . and she must be . . . the right sort of wife you . . . should have."

The Earl reached out his hand and took Purilla's in his.

He felt her tremble because he was touching her, but his fingers merely tightened on hers and he said quietly:

"You are the 'right sort of wife' I have always envisaged bearing my name and being beside me for the rest of my life."

He felt Purilla stiffen. Then she said:

"Is that true . . . really . . . true?"

"I swear it is," the Earl answered, "and although I have known a number of charming ladies who have been kind enough to show me their affection, I have never, until I met you, asked one to marry me."

"But . . . but you only . . . married me," Purilla said in a very small voice, "so that you did . . . not have to marry . . . Lady Louise."

"I think that even if there had been no Lady Louise in my life," the Earl said, "fate would have brought us together somehow. I should have known that you were my 'Golden Fleece' for whom I have been searching, although I was not really aware of it until now."

"Do you . . . mean that?"

He could barely hear the words, and yet the

expression in Purilla's eyes as she looked at him spoke more eloquently than anything she said.

For a moment the Earl seemed to be trying to find the right reply. Then he answered:

"Because it is important in our married life that we should be honest with each other, I thought when I first saw you that you were one of the most attractive people I had ever met. But I believed that what you wanted, and what you told me everyone sought for, as if it were the Golden Fleece, was beyond my capabilities."

Purilla did not speak but he felt her fingers move beneath his and went on:

"Then as we talked together on subjects I never expected to discuss with a woman, when every day I was at the Manor I realised how sweet, pure, and lovely you were, and while I was still trying wildly to escape from the trap Lady Louise had set for me, simply because I had inherited my uncle's title, I knew you would make me exactly the wife I wanted."

The Earl's voice was harsh as he added:

"She had no real interest in me while I was just an officer in the Grenadiers, and I doubt if she would ever have given me a thought if we had not met again casually in one of the Royal Residences."

He knew Purilla was listening intently as he continued:

"I shrank in horror from the idea of having a wife who wanted to marry me merely because of my social position and my possessions. Then fate sent you to save me at almost the eleventh hour."

"I am ... glad I ... could do ... that," Purilla murmured, "but I wish you had ... told me the ... difficulty you were in."

"I meant to do so sooner or later," the Earl answered, "but it did not seem particularly important, and I thought it might spoil your happiness and perhaps destroy the love I thought you were beginning to give me."

He spoke very gently and he knew that he startled her, and once again she blushed and turned her face away from him.

"Even when we were married," the Earl said, "I knew that the Duke, on the instigation of his daughter, could make things very difficult and unpleasant for me and perhaps for you."

"That is why you ... pretended we had been ... married before you ... inherited the title," Purilla said.

"Exactly," the Earl agreed, "and now that the Duke has accepted the situation, there will be nothing he can do to discredit me. So now we can start our married life without there being any unpleasantness."

As he spoke, the Earl thought that it would be difficult to explain to Purilla how differently he felt about everything.

He thought that his whole outlook had changed since he had watched the Duke and Lady Louise drive away and knew that they were driving out of his life forever.

Now he could start a new chapter of a new life, and, holding Purilla's hand as they lay in the candlelit bed, he knew it would be the most exciting thing that had ever happened to him.

Aloud he said:

"Now that that is out of our way, I want you to tell me how you managed to make me aware of what had happened to you."

"You really ... knew I was in danger?" Purilla gasped, turning her face to him again.

"I was certain of it in my heart," the Earl replied.

"It worked ... it really worked!" Purilla murmured as if to herself.

"Tell me exactly what happened."

Purilla told him how Jason had chased a rabbit into the cave and, because he did not hear her calling him, she had gone into the cave herself to try to get him out.

"Then the chalk fell down and blocked the entrance," she said, "so I knew that we were trapped."

"What did you do?"

"I was frightened ... very frightened," she replied, "and I thought perhaps you would never ...

find me, and Jason and I would...die of the... cold."

There was a little throb in her voice which made him know that she was not far from tears.

He moved nearer to her and put his arm round her as he had done when he had carried her home on the front of his horse.

He felt her quiver, then her head fell back against his shoulder and he was sure that her heart was beating frantically.

"Go on with what you were telling me," he said.

"I...remember...how we talked about the Indians having...supernatural ways of...communicating with each other, and Richard had told me he had seen evidence of it among the men he... commanded."

"So what did you do?"

"I...called to...you and...prayed for you to...come and...rescue me."

The Earl drew her a little closer still.

"I heard you," he said. "I could feel you beside me, pleading with me, telling me something, and I knew you were in danger."

Purilla gave a sigh of happiness.

"It is so...wonderful to think that I could get in...touch with you like...that. I felt as if I were sending you a message...on wings."

"And you were certain that I would hear you?"

"I was sure you would...I believed that if I could...reach you...you would...understand."

"Did you ask yourself why I should understand," the Earl enquired, "as perhaps no other man would have been able to?"

Purilla raised her face to look at him in a puzzled manner and he said very softly:

"I think what you are saying is that you sent me your love."

Her eyes fell before his and she would have turned her head away if he had not held her chin captive with his free hand.

"You spoke to me with love," he said, "and I

listened with love. That is why I was able to save you."

"With ... l-love?"

He could barely hear the words, and yet he knew what she said.

"I love you, my darling! I was so, foolish not to have told you so before, but I did not realise myself how much you meant to me or how much I loved you until I knew you were in danger."

"Y-you ... love me?"

He saw the radiance in her eyes and heard the lilt in her voice.

"I love you in exactly the way you wanted me to," the Earl said. "I have found my Golden Fleece, Purilla, and I understand all the things you have been trying to tell me, which I was too obtuse and too stupid to comprehend! Now nothing else is of any importance."

As he spoke he pulled her still nearer to him.

He was very gentle and he knew as his lips touched hers that they were exactly as he had thought they would be, soft, sweet, innocent like the petals of a lily, and just as lovely.

The Earl knew that the reason why he had been so slow in recognising that in Purilla he had found the woman he wanted as his wife, was that his feelings for her were a rapture and a glory he had never known before.

What he felt for Purilla was like the emotions that were aroused on hearing celestial music or looking at the beauty of the sun.

Then because she was so lovely and he knew that the sensations he aroused in her were an ecstasy that came from Heaven itself, the Earl knew he was blessed as few men are in finding perfection.

His lips became more possessive, more insistent, and as he knew that Purilla responded not only with her body but with her heart and her soul, he told himself that he would love and protect her from everything that was ugly and wicked for the rest of their lives.

He raised his head to look down at the happiness that had transformed her face so that she radiated a beauty that was unbelievable.

"I love you!" he said. "Now tell me what you feel for me."

"I...I love...you...I love...you!" Purilla cried. "I have loved you from the first moment I... saw you...and I knew you were the man who had...always been in my...dreams."

"My darling! That is what I wanted you to say," the Earl replied, "and I will love you from now until eternity, and perhaps in a million lives that will come after this one."

"I cannot...believe that you really...love me," Purilla whispered.

"Then that is something I shall have to prove to you and to myself," the Earl answered, "because until I met you, I never knew that love was like this or that it could be so wonderful."

"It was...love that made you...hear me when I called you, and you do believe...now that such things are...possible?"

"I not only believe," the Earl said, "but you and I will explore them, believe in them, and, where it is possible, try them for ourselves."

Purilla gave a little cry of delight, and he added:

"I knew you were in danger, and when I reflect I might not have found you, it makes me afraid to ever let you out of my sight again."

"It was...foolish of me not to have anticipated that the cave might be dangerous," Purilla admitted. "At the same time, in a way I am glad it happened, because now we know we can...reach each other even when we are apart and that our love is... stronger than...time and space."

"I know that now," the Earl said, "and because I believe, my precious one, as you do, that our love comes from God, we will work to use our instincts and our happiness to help other people. That is something you have already shown me is important."

"How can you be so marvellous?" Purilla asked.

"I am happy . . . so very . . . very happy, and I will thank God every minute of every day of my life that you are my . . . husband."

The last word was lost against the Earl's lips as he was kissing her once again.

As he held her closer and still closer against him until she could feel the beating of his heart, she knew that she excited him and that he did really love her as she wanted to be loved.

She could feel a strange fire on the Earl's lips and in his kisses that made her feel as if he drew her heart from her body and made it his.

At the same time, she wanted to give him not only her heart but her whole self so that she no longer existed as a separate person but became a part of him.

She did not understand what she wanted, except that it was very wonderful, and the sensations he aroused in her seemed to be part of the beauty with which they were surrounded and the glory of the sun.

"I love you so much," the Earl was saying, "that I am afraid of frightening you, my darling one, and I am trying to be very gentle."

"I am . . . not frightened," Purilla replied, "and you fill the whole world and the sky until there is nothing but you . . . and love."

There was just a touch of awe in her voice which the Earl found very moving.

As he kissed her again he felt as if they were both swept into the sky.

The love Purilla had brought him was so ecstatic and at the same time so pure and sacred that he wanted to go down on his knees and worship her for giving him the Golden Fleece which all men seek but only a few are lucky enough to find.

Then as he felt her quiver against him, he knew she was not only Divine but very human, and that to teach her about love would thrill, excite, and intrigue him for the rest of his life.

"I love my wonderful little wife! I love you!"

His voice was hoarse and the sincerity with which he spoke brought the tears to Purilla's eyes.

Then there was only the closeness of two people whose love needed no words because their thoughts, minds, hearts, souls, and bodies made them one for all eternity.

ABOUT THE AUTHOR

BARBARA CARTLAND, the world's most famous romantic novelist, who is also an historian, playwright, lecturer, political speaker and television personality, has now written over 200 books.

She has also had many historical works published and has written four autobiographies as well as the biographies of her mother and that of her brother Ronald Cartland, who was the first Member of Parliament to be killed in the last war. This book has a preface by Sir Winston Churchill.

Barbara Cartland has sold 100 million books over the world, more than half of these in the U.S.A. She broke the world record in 1975 by writing twenty books, and her own record in 1976 with twenty-one. In addition, her album of love songs has just been published, sung with the Royal Philharmonic Orchestra.

In private life, Barbara Cartland, who is a Dame of the Order of St. John of Jerusalem, has fought for better conditions and salaries for Midwives and Nurses. As President of the Royal College of Midwives (Hertfordshire Branch), she has been invested with the first Badge of Office ever given in Great Britain which was subscribed to by the Midwives themselves. She has also championed the cause for old people and founded the first Romany Gypsy Camp in the world.

Barbara Cartland is deeply interested in Vitamin Therapy and is President of the British National Association for Health.

ROMANTIC TOURS
inspired by
BARBARA CARTLAND

With the same research and care that goes into the writing of her novels, Barbara Cartland has designed a series of tours to the romantic and exciting places you have read about in her books.

- You will meet the author herself in her home, Camfield Place.
- You will lunch with the Earl and Countess Spencer (Barbara Cartland's daughter) at their home Althorp Park.
- You will spend one unforgettable week touring England with special events arranged for you wherever you go.

All this is offered to you plus second optional weeks to such other historic and exotic destinations as SCOTLAND AND WALES, FRANCE, AUSTRIA AND GERMANY, TURKEY, EGYPT AND INDIA.

PRESENTED IN COOPERATION WITH
THE WORLD OF OZ AND BRITISH AIRWAYS

Send for your Romantic Tours folder now! Don't miss the opportunity of sharing this unique travel experience with other admirers and fans of BARBARA CARTLAND.